BA
WER   ,
VAMPIRES,

AND OTHER CREATURES OF THE NIGHT

BANSHEES, WEREWOLVES, VAMPIRES,

AND OTHER CREATURES OF THE NIGHT

*Facts, Fictions, and
First-Hand Accounts*

VARLA VENTURA

WEISERBOOKS
San Francisco, CA / Newburyport, MA

First published in 2013 by Weiser Books, an imprint of
Red Wheel/Weiser, LLC
With offices at:
665 Third Street, Suite 400
San Francisco, CA 94107
www.redwheelweiser.com

Library of Congress Cataloging-in-Publication Data

Ventura, Varla, 1958-
    Banshees, werewolves, vampires, and other creatures of the night : facts,
fictions, and first-hand accounts / Varla Ventura.
        pages cm.
    ISBN 978-1-57863-547-4 (pbk.)
    1. Werewolves. 2. Vampires. 3. Banshees. I. Title.
    GR830.W4V46 2013
    398.24'54—dc23   2013022148

Cover design by Jim Warner
Interior by Dutton & Sherman Design
Typeset in Adobe Caslon text and Historical FellType display

Printed in the United States of America
TS

10 9 8 7 6 5 4 3 2 1

The paper used in this publication meets the minimum requirements of the
American National Standard for Information Sciences—Permanence of Paper for
Printed Library Materials Z39.48-1992 (R1997).

For Wendy the Witch

CONTENTS

PART ONE: BANSHEES

PART TWO: WEREWOLVES

PART THREE: VAMPIRES

BLOODY APPENDICES

INTRODUCTION

Things That Go Bump in the Night

Some things have to be believed to be seen.

—Ralph Hodgson

Many a lonesome night has been spent listening with trepidation to the howl of the wind. In spite of our rational minds and our sound judgment, there is nearly always—especially in that passage of time between midnight and three in the morning—a sound that simply cannot be explained away. Oh, but we try. To the rattle of the windowpane and the thump upon the porch we say, "'Tis only the wind!" To the squeak of the floorboards and the bang on the roof we declare, "This old house is settling!" But deep inside, and we have all likely felt it at one time or another, there is an uneasy understanding that something very supernatural is afoot.

Ever since we could build huts or lay straw in caves, we've lived in awe and fear of the world outside the circle of the campfire's light. While some legends were born to keep children close or to explain not-yet-known diseases, others have no known origin, their stories as old and immortal as a vampire's glint.

About a year ago, my publisher asked me to start digging around in old volumes of forgotten lore to collect stories about magical creatures and the paranormal. These findings became the blueprint for this book (as well as my book *Among the Mermaids*). As I jumped from one dusty volume to another, reading ghost stories, vampire tales, and lycanthropic laments, I discovered many connections between the stories. Most of the works I found to be compelling were written around the same time—in the late 19th and early 20th centuries—so it is not surprising that they have a certain number of similarities. For example, Elliott O'Donnell, author of several stories in this collection, quotes D.R. McAnally Jr., another author whom I found to be an expert in his field of banshees and ghosts. William Butler Yeats, known today not just as a poet but also a leading expert in Irish folklore, drew heavily upon the works of T. Crofton Croker and William Wirt Sikes—both of whom have found homes throughout this collection. And you will no doubt be as excited as I was to discover the connection between Mary Shelley's *Frankenstein* and the first vampire novel published in English—John William Polidori's *The Vampyre*, published some seventy years before Bram Stoker's *Dracula*. Oh yes, and you'll also enjoy a posthumously published story by Stoker himself. And these masters of folklore, amateur anthropologists, and sociologists all had one thing in common: they could not, beyond a shadow of all doubt, declare that the supernatural did not exist. Ultimately, they agree (as do I) that there are creatures out there that simply defy logic.

So as you are settling in with this book, dimming your lights a bit, perhaps stoking the fire, I would encourage you to remember the very good odds that what you are afraid of is likely justified. Is it a branch on the glass, or the claw of the werewolf? A neighboring dog, or a thundering beast that slipped beyond the moonlight at the meadow's edge? Vampires, ghosts, werewolves, banshees—there are many, many things out there clawing in the night, snarling in the shadows. So lock your door, draw your curtains, and read on! I hope this book brings you terror and delight.

Varla Ventura
San Francisco, 2013

Part One

BANSHEES

Banshees, whether good or bad, are just as individual as any member of the family they haunt.

—Elliott O'Donnell

A Kiss in the Dreamhouse

One of my favorite bands as a young, surly teen was Siouxsie and the Banshees, whose front woman Siouxsie Sioux was a gothic enchantress who howled like a mythological siren, luring you in with her tales of travel and woe. So when I came upon stories like Elliott O'Donnell's "Malevolent Banshees" and T. "Soul Cages" Crofton Croker's banshee legend, I simply had to dust off the old vinyl and paint on some heavy eyeliner so I could have a good ol' fashioned Banshee Bash.

Banshees are among the most feared creatures of the fairy kingdom, and this may be in part to the sympathies they invoke when you hear their wailing. You could easily be lured into the dark of night, hoping to help the pathetic creature who sounds as if she is in mourning. Some tales recount that banshees are the ghosts of women who have died in childbirth; others say they are the restless spirits of unrequited lovers. Most banshees are passed down from generation to generation within a family, though their presence can be brought on at any time.

One thing is certain: not all banshees are created equal. The more common sad and beautiful banshee is not the only type. There is another species of banshee known as the malevolent banshee. This is a banshee that screeches in a different pitch, and who will blow in on the wind and leave your kitchen upended and your heart nearly expired. If you are able to actually survive an encounter with one of these creatures, you will be left with shattered teacups, bulging eyes, and sickened nerves that you may never recover from.

In this first section, I'll share some of my favorite banshee facts and fictions, and perhaps you, too, will find yourself ready to howl, wail, and ultimately cower from the song of the banshee.

I

READY TO PLAY
NOT-SO-NICE

In this world, there is always danger for those who are afraid of it.

—GEORGE BERNARD SHAW

Elliott O'Donnell was an Irish author who wrote more than forty books on ghosts, paranormal encounters, and creatures of the fairy race. Unlike so many authors of his time who conducted psychic experiments, and who often took the skeptical or sensational point of view, O'Donnell had a more authentic approach to ghost stories. He claimed to have numerous encounters himself, including with a ghost when he was five years old. He also reported having been strangled by a phantom somewhere in Dublin. A descendant of ancient Irish chieftains (most notably King Arthur), O'Donnell attended Clifton College in Bristol and Queen's Service

Academy in Dublin, where he received a superior education. After traveling to America and becoming a policeman, he returned to England, where he trained for the theater and later served in the British army during World War I.

Eventually, he found his calling as a ghost hunter. During this time, his books about true ghost stories and hauntings increased in popularity, bolstering his reputation as the authority on the paranormal. O'Donnell once said, "I have investigated, sometimes alone, and sometimes with other people and the press, many cases of reputed hauntings. I believe in ghosts but am not a spiritualist." I've chosen to keep his irregular capitalization of the word *banshee* throughout the following piece, "The Malevolent Banshee" (just as I've kept the authors' original spellings of creature names throughout the book). I think it speaks to his belief and to the importance of these creatures in his writings. In fact, in the following essay on banshees, O'Donnell reveals that his own kin have a banshee, a familial ghost that warns of death.

And take heart, dear reader, for O'Donnell survived his banshee encounters! Perhaps the banshee you encounter will be more of the sad variety, and you will survive with lightly shattered nerves and a haunting melody that will never leave your head. Ever.

The Malevolent Banshee
by Elliott O'Donnell

I will now present to the reader a few equally authentic accounts of malevolent or unfriendly Banshees. Before doing so, however, I would like to call attention to the fact that, once when I was reading a paper on Banshees before the Irish Literary Society, in Hanover Square, a lady got up and, challenging my remark that not all Banshees were alike, tried to prove that I was wrong, on the assumption that all Banshees must be sad and beautiful because the Banshee in her family happened to be sad and beautiful, an argument, if argument it can be called, which, although it is a fairly common one, cannot, of course, be taken seriously.

Moreover, as I have already stated, there is abundant evidence to show that Banshees are of many and diverse kinds; and that no two appear to be exactly alike or to act in precisely the same fashion.

According to Mr. McAnally, the malevolent Banshee is invariably "a horrible hag with ugly, distorted features; maledictions are written in every line of her wrinkled face, and her outstretched arms call down curses on the doomed member of the hated race."

Other writers, too, would seem more or less to encourage the idea that all malignant Banshees are cast in one mould and all beautiful Banshees in another, whereas from my own personal experiences I should say that Banshees, whether good or bad, are just as individual as any member of the family they haunt.

It is related of a certain ancient Mayo family that a chief of the race once made love to a very beautiful girl whom he betrayed and subsequently murdered. With her dying breath the girl cursed her murderer and swore she would haunt him and his forever. Years rolled by; the cruel deceiver married, and, with the passing away of all who knew him in his youth, he came to be regarded as a model of absolute propriety and rectitude. Hence it was in these circumstances that he was sitting one night before a big blazing fire in the hall of his castle, outwardly happy enough and surrounded by his sons and daughters, when loud shrieks of exultation were heard coming, it seemed, from someone who was standing on the path close to the castle walls. All rushed out to see who it was, but no one was there, and the grounds, as far as the eye could reach, were absolutely deserted.

Later on, however, some little time after the household had retired to rest, the same demoniacal disturbances took place; peal after peal of wild, malicious laughter rang out, followed by a discordant moaning and screaming. This time the aged chieftain did not accompany the rest of the household in their search for the originator of the disturbances. Possibly, in that discordant moaning and screaming he fancied he could detect the voice of the murdered girl; and, possibly, accepting the manifestation as a death-warning, he was not surprised on the following day, when he was waylaid out of doors and brutally done to death by one of his followers.

Needless to say, perhaps, the haunting of this Banshee still continues, the same phenomena occurring at least once to every generation of the family, before the death of one of its members. Happily, however, the haunting now does not necessarily precede a violent death, and in this respect, though in this respect only, differs from the original.

Another haunting by this same species of Banshee was brought to my notice the last time I was in Ireland. I happened to be visiting a certain relative of mine, at that date residing in Black Rock, and from her I learned the following, which now appears in print for the first time.

About the middle of the last century, when my relative was in her teens, some friends of hers, the O'D.'s, were living in a big old-fashioned country house, somewhere between Ballinanty and Hospital in the County of Limerick. The family consisted of Mr O'D., who had been something in India in his youth and was now very much of a recluse, though much esteemed locally on account of his extreme piety and good-heartedness; Mrs O'D., who, despite her grey hair and wrinkled countenance, still retained traces of more than ordinary good looks; Wilfred, a handsome but decidedly headstrong young man of between twenty-five and thirty; and Ellen, a blue-eyed, golden-haired girl of the true Milesian type of Irish beauty.

My relative was on terms of the greatest intimacy with the whole family, but especially with the two younger folk, and it was generally expected that she and Wilfred would make what is vulgarly termed a "match of it." Indeed, the first of the ghostly happenings that she experienced in connection with the O'D.'s actually occurred the very day Wilfred took the long-anticipated step and proposed to her.

It seems that my relative was out for a walk one afternoon with Ellen and Wilfred, when the latter, taking advantage of his sister's sudden fancy for going on ahead to look for dog-roses, passionately declared his love, and, apparently, did not declare it in vain. The trio, then, in more or less exalted spirits—for my relative had of course let Ellen into the secret—walked home together, and as they were passing through a big wooden gateway into the garden at the rear of the O'D.'s house, they perceived a tall, spare woman, with her back towards them, digging away furiously.

"Hullo," Wilfred exclaimed, "who's that?"

"I don't know," Ellen replied. "It's certainly not Mary" (Mary was the old cook who, like many of the servants of that period, did not confine her labour to the culinary art, but performed all kinds of odd jobs as well), "nor anyone from the farm. But what on earth does she think she's doing? Hey, there!" and Ellen, raising her naturally sweet and musical voice, gave a little shout.

The woman instantly turned round, and the trio received a most violent shock. The light was fading, for it was late in the afternoon, but what little there was seemed to be entirely concentrated on the visage before them, making it appear luminous. It was a broad face with very pronounced cheekbones; a large mouth, the thin lips of which were fixed in a dreadful and mocking leer; and very pale, obliquely set eyes that glowed banefully as they met the gaze of the three now appalled spectators.

For some seconds the evil-looking creature stood in dead silence, apparently gloating over the discomposure her appearance had produced, and, then, suddenly shouldering her spade, she walked slowly away, turning round every now and again to cast the same malevolent gleeful look at them, until she came to the hedge that separated the garden from a long disused stone quarry, when she seemed suddenly to fade away in the now very uncertain twilight, and disappear.

For some moments no one spoke or stirred, but continued gazing after her in a kind of paralysed astonishment. Wilfred was the first to break the silence.

"What an awful looking hag," he exclaimed. "Where's she gone?"

Ellen whistled. "Ask another," she said. "There's nowhere she could have gone excepting into the quarry, and my only hope is that she is lying at the bottom of it with a broken neck, for I certainly never wish to see her again. But come, let's be moving on, I'm chilly."

> *"What an awful looking hag," he exclaimed. "Where's she gone?"*

They started off, but had only proceeded a few yards, when, apparently from the direction of the quarry, came a peal of laughter, so mocking and malignant and altogether evil, that all three involuntarily quickened their steps, and, at the same time, refrained from speaking, until they had reached the house, which they hastily entered, securely closing the door behind them. They then went straight to Mr O'D. and asked him who the old woman was whom they had just seen.

"What was she like?" he queried. "I haven't authorised anyone but Mary to go into the garden."

"It certainly wasn't Mary," Ellen responded quickly. "It was some hideous old crone who was digging away like anything. On our approach she left off and gave us the most diabolical look I have ever seen. Then she went away and seemed to vanish in the hedge by the quarry. We afterwards heard her give the most appalling and intensely evil laugh that you can imagine. Whoever is she?"

"I can't think," Mr O'D. replied, looking somewhat unusually pale. "It is no one whom I know. Very possibly she was a tramp or gipsy. We must take care to keep all the doors locked. Whatever you do, don't mention a word about her to your mother or to Mary—they are both nervous and very easily frightened."

All three promised, and the matter was then allowed to drop, but my relative, who returned home before it got quite dark, subsequently learned that that night, some time after the O'D. household had all retired to rest, peal after peal of the same infernal mocking laughter was heard, just under the windows, first of all in the front of the house, and then in the rear; and that, on the morrow, came the news that the business concern in which most of Mr O'D.'s money was invested had gone smash and the family were practically penniless.

The house now was in imminent danger of being sold, and many people thought that it was merely to avert this catastrophe and to enable her parents to keep a roof over their heads that Ellen accepted the attentions of a very vulgar parvenu (an Englishman) in Limerick, and eventually married him. Where there is no love, however, there is never any happiness, and where there is not even "liking," there is very often hate; and in Ellen's case hate there was without any doubt. Barely able, even from the first, to tolerate her husband (his favourite trick was to make love to her in public and almost in the same breath bully her—also in public), she eventually grew to loathe him, and at last, unable to endure his hated presence any longer, she eloped with an officer who was stationed in the neighbourhood. The night before Ellen took this step, my relative and Wilfred (the latter was escorting his fiancée home after a pleasant evening spent in her company) again heard the malevolent laughter, which (although they could see no one) pursued them for some distance along the moonlit lanes and across the common leading to the spot where my relative lived. After this the laughter was not heard again for two years, but at the end of that period my relative had another experience of the phenomena.

She was again spending the evening with the O'D.'s, and, on this occasion, she was discussing with Mr and Mrs O'D. the advent of Wilfred, who was expected to arrive home from the West Indies any time within the next few days. My relative was not unnaturally interested, as it had been arranged that she and Wilfred should marry, as soon as possible after his arrival in Ireland. They were all three—Mr and Mrs O'D. and my relative—engaged in animated conversation (the old people had unexpectedly come into a little money, and that, too, had considerably contributed to their cheerfulness), when Mrs O'D., fancying she heard someone calling to her from the garden, got up and went to the window.

"Harry," she exclaimed, still looking out and apparently unable to remove her gaze, "do come. There's the most awful old woman in the garden, staring hard at me. Quick, both of you. She's perfectly horrible; she frightens me."

My relative and Mr O'D. at once sprang up and hastened to her side, and, there, they saw, gazing up at them, the pallor of its cheeks intensified by a stray moonbeam which seemed to be concentrated solely on it, a face which my relative recognised immediately as that of the woman she had seen, two years ago, digging in the garden. The old hag seemed to remember my relative, too, for, as their glances met, a gleam of recognition crept into her light eyes, and, a moment later, gave way to an expression of such diabolical hate that my relative involuntarily caught hold of Mr O'D. for protection. Evidently noting this action the creature leered horribly, and then, drawing a kind of shawl or hood tightly over its head, moved away with a kind of gliding motion, vanishing round an angle of the wall.

Mr O'D. at once went out into the garden, but, after a few minutes, returned, declaring that, although he had searched in every direction, not a trace of their sinister-looking visitor could he see anywhere. He had hardly, however, finished speaking, when, apparently from close to the house, came several peals of the most hellish laughter, that terminated in one loud, prolonged wail, unmistakably ominous and menacing.

"Oh, Harry," Mrs O'D. exclaimed, on the verge of fainting, "what can be the meaning of it? That was surely no living woman."

"No," Mr O'D. replied slowly, "it was the Banshee. As you know, the O'D. Banshee, for some reason or another, possesses an inveterate hatred of my family, and we must prepare again for some evil tidings. But," he went on, steadying his voice with an effort, "with God's grace we must face it, for whatever happens it is His Divine will."

A few days later my relative, as may be imagined, was immeasurably shocked to hear that Mr O'D. had been sent word that Wilfred was dead. He had, it appeared, been stricken down with fever, supposed to have been caught from one of his fellow-passengers, and had died on the very day that he should have landed, on the very day, in fact (as it was afterwards ascertained from a comparison of dates), upon which his parents and fiancée, together, had heard and seen the Banshee.

It has been said that a banshee is really the disembodied soul of someone who once lived and was attached to the family in some way. It depends upon the relationship that the banshee had with the dying family member as to how the banshee announces his or her coming death. If the person about to die was of a gentle, kind disposition, then the banshee will appear and sing soft songs of warning, summoning the person to death. But if the person destined to die was of a hateful disposition, then the banshee will make her announcement with horrible cries and screams.

—Raymond Buckland, from *The Weiser Field Guide to Ghosts*

Soon after this unhappy event my relative left the neighbourhood and went to live with some friends near Dublin, and though, from time to time, she corresponded with the O'D.'s, she never again heard anything of their Banshee.

This same relative of mine, whom I will now call Miss S—— (she never married), was acquainted with two old maiden ladies named O'Rorke who, many years ago, lived in a semi-detached house close to Lower Merrion Street. Miss S—— did not know to what branch of the O'Rorkes they belonged, for they were very reticent with regard to their family history, but she believed they originally came from the south-west and were distantly connected with some of her own people.

With regard to their house, there certainly was something peculiar, since in it was one room that was invariably kept locked, and in connection with this room it was said there existed a mystery of the most frightful and harrowing description.

My relative often had it on the tip of her tongue to refer to the room, just to see what effect it would have on the two old ladies, but she could never quite sum up the courage to do so. One afternoon, however, when she was calling on them, the subject was brought to their notice in a very startling manner.

The elder of the two sisters, Miss Georgina, who was presiding at the tea table, had just handed Miss S—— a cup of tea and was about to pour out another for herself, when into the room, with her cap all awry and her eyes bulging, rushed one of the servants.

"Good gracious!" Miss Georgina exclaimed, "whatever's the matter, Bridget?"

"Matter!" Bridget retorted, in a brogue which I will not attempt to imitate. "Why, someone's got into that room you always keep locked and is making the devil of a noise, enough to raise all the Saints in Heaven. Norah" (Norah was the cook) "and I both heard it—a groaning, and a chuckling, and a scratching, as if the cratur was tearing up the boards and breaking all the furniture, and all the while keening and laughing. For the love of Heaven, ladies, come and hear it for yourselves. Such goings on! Ochone! Ochone!"

Both ladies, Miss S—— said, turned deadly pale, and Miss Harriet, the younger sister, was on the brink of tears.

"Where is cook?" Miss Georgina, who was by far the stronger minded of the two, suddenly said, addressing Bridget. "If she is upstairs, tell her to come down at once. Miss Harriet and I will go and see what the noise is that you complain about upstairs. There really is no need to make all this disturbance"—here she assumed an air of the utmost severity—"it's sure to be either mice or rats."

"Mice or rats!" Bridget echoed. "I'm sorry for the mice and rats as make all those noises. 'Tis some evil spirit, sure, and Norah is of the same mind," and with those parting words she slammed the door behind her.

The sisters, then, begging to be excused for a few minutes, left the room, and returned shortly afterwards looking terribly white and distressed.

"I am sure you must think all this very odd," Miss Georgina observed with as great a degree of unconcern as she could assume, "and I feel we owe you an explanation, but I must beg you will not repeat a word of what we tell you to anyone else."

Miss S—— promised she would not, and then composed herself to listen.

"We have in our family," Miss O'Rorke began, "a most unpleasant attachment; in other words, a most unpleasant Banshee. Being Irish, you will not laugh, of course, as many English people do, at what I say. You know as well as I do, perhaps, that many of the really ancient Irish families possess Banshees."

Miss S—— nodded. "We have one ourselves," she remarked, "but pray go on. I am intensely interested."

"Well, unlike most of the Banshees," Miss Georgina continued, "ours is appallingly ugly and malevolent; so frightful, indeed, that to see it, even, is sometimes fatal. One of our great-great-uncles, for instance, to whom it once appeared, is reported to have died from shock; a similar fate overtaking another of our ancestors, who also saw it. Fortunately, it seems to have a strong attraction in the shape of an old gold ring which has been in the possession of the family from time immemorial. Both ancestors I have referred to are alleged to have been wearing this ring at the time the Banshee appeared to them, and it is said to strictly confine its manifestations to the immediate vicinity of that article. That is why our parents always kept the ring strictly isolated, in a locked room, the key of which was never, for a moment, allowed to be out of their possession. And we have strenuously followed their example. That is the explanation of the mystery you have doubtless heard about, for I believe—thanks to the servants—it has become the gossip of half Dublin."

"And the noise Bridget referred to," Miss S—— ventured to remark, somewhat timidly, "was that the Banshee?"

Miss Georgina nodded.

"I fear it was," she observed solemnly, "and that we shall shortly hear of a relative's death or grave catastrophe to some member of the family; probably, a cousin of ours in County Galway, who has been ill for some weeks, is dying."

She was partly right, although the latter surmise was not correct. Within a few days of the Banshee's visit a member of the family died, but it was not the sick cousin, it was Miss Georgina's own sister, Harriet!

2

IRISH WONDERS

If you're lucky enough to be Irish, you're lucky enough.

—Old Irish Saying

In Elliott O'Donnell's previous essay, D.R. McAnally Jr. is quoted as thinking the worst about the Banshee. Though his family emigrated from Ireland, their history indicates they were of historically Scottish descent. David Rice McAnally. Jr. wrote *Irish Wonders: The Ghosts, Giants, Pookas, Demons, Leprechawns, Banshees, Fairies, Witches, Widows, Old Maids, and Other Marvels of the Emerald Isle* in 1888. Little is known about McAnally. The son of an Episcopalian minister, he taught English literature at Missouri State University (now the University of Missouri) in Columbia, circa 1877. Perhaps this Methodist background brings the strong measure of (unlike O'Donnell) a less-than-favorable view of the superstitious creatures and the people who believed them. His tone is undeniably one of disbelief, and a bit ethnocentric. Still, his writings contain some of the best examples of as-told-to accounts of banshees, pookas, witches, and other magical creatures.

The Banshee
by D.R. McAnally Jr.

Although the Irish have the reputation of being grossly superstitious, they are not a whit more so than the peasantry of England, France, or Germany, nor scarcely as much addicted to superstitious beliefs and fancies as the lower class of Scottish Highlanders. The Irish imagination is, however, so lively as to endow the legends of the Emerald Isle with an individuality not possessed by those of most other nations, while the Irish command of language presents the creatures of Hibernian fancy in a garb so vividly real and yet so fantastically original as to make an impression sometimes exceedingly startling.

Of the creations of the Irish imagination, some are humorous, some grotesque, and some awe-inspiring even to sublimity, and chief among the last class is "the weird-wailing Banshee, that sings by night her mournful cry," giving notice to the family she attends that one of its members is soon to be called to the spirit-world. The name of this dreaded attendant is variously pronounced, as Banshee, Banshi, and Benshee, being translated by different scholars, the Female Fairy, the Woman of Peace, the Lady of Death, the Angel of Death, the White Lady of Sorrow, the Nymph of the Air, and the Spirit of the Air. The Banshee is quite distinct from the Fearshee or Shifra, the Man of Peace, the latter bringing good tidings and singing a joyful lay near the house when unexpected good fortune is to befall any or all its inmates. The Banshee is really a disembodied soul, that of one who, in life, was strongly attached to the family, or who had good reason to hate all its members. Thus, in different instances, the Banshee's song may be inspired by opposite motives. When the Banshee loves those whom she calls, the song is a low, soft chant, giving notice, indeed, of the close proximity of the angel of death, but with a tenderness of tone that reassures the one destined to die and comforts the survivors; rather a welcome than a warning, and having in its tones a thrill of exultation, as though the messenger spirit were bringing glad tidings to him summoned to join the waiting throng of his ancestors. If, during her lifetime, the Banshee was an enemy of the family, the cry is the scream of a fiend, howling with demoniac delight over the coming death-agony of another of her foes.

In some parts of Ireland there exists a belief that the spirits of the dead are not taken from earth, nor do they lose all their former interest in earthly affairs, but enjoy the happiness of the saved, or suffer the punishment imposed for their sins, in the neighborhood of the scenes among which they lived while clothed in flesh and blood. At particular crises in the affairs of mortals, these disenthralled spirits sometimes display joy or grief in such a manner as to attract the attention of living men and women. At weddings they are frequently unseen guests; at funerals they are always present; and sometimes, at both weddings and funerals, their presence is recognized by aerial voices or mysterious music known to be of unearthly origin. The spirits of the good wander with the living as guardian angels, but the spirits of the bad are restrained in their action, and compelled to do penance at or near the places where their crimes were committed. Some are chained at the bottoms of the lakes, others buried under ground, others confined in mountain gorges; some hang on the sides of precipices, others are transfixed on the tree-tops, while others haunt the homes of their ancestors, all waiting till the penance has been endured and the hour of release arrives. The Castle of Dunseverick, in Antrim, is believed to be still inhabited by the spirit of a chief, who there atones for a horrid crime, while the castles of Dunluce, of Magrath, and many others are similarly peopled by the wicked dead. In the Abbey of Clare, the ghost of a sinful abbot walks and will continue to do so until his sin has been atoned for by the prayers he unceasingly mutters in his tireless march up and down the aisles of the ruined nave.

The Banshee is of the spirits who look with interested eyes on earthly doings; and, deeply attached to the old families, or, on the contrary, regarding all their members with a hatred beyond that known to mortals, lingers about their dwellings to soften or to aggravate the sorrow of the approaching death. The Banshee attends only the old families, and though their descendants, through misfortune, may be brought down from high estate to the ranks of peasant-tenants, she never leaves nor forgets them till the last member has been gathered to his fathers in the churchyard. The MacCarthys, Magraths, O'Neills, O'Rileys, O'Sullivans, O'Reardons, O'Flahertys, and almost all other old families of Ireland, have Banshees, though many representatives of these names are in abject poverty.

One of the best known Irish ghosts is the banshee (*bean sidhe*), a harbinger of death. The name means "woman of the mounds" or "female fairy." Sir Walter Scott said, "The distinction of a Banshee is only allowed to families of the pure Milesian stock, and is never ascribed to any descendant of the proudest Norman or the boldest Saxon who followed the banner of Earl Strongbow, much less to adventurers of later dates who have obtained settlements in the Green Isle." He would have one believe, therefore, that only the purest, oldest, and highest born of the Irish are ever visited by a banshee. Certainly the O'Rourkes, O'Brians, O'Malleys, and the O'Donnals—all great families—have been visited by the banshee over several generations.

—Raymond Buckland, from *The Weiser Field Guide to Ghosts*

The song of the Banshee is commonly heard a day or two before the death of which it gives notice, though instances are cited of the song at the beginning of a course of conduct or line of undertaking that resulted fatally. Thus, in Kerry, a young girl engaged herself to a youth, and at the moment her promise of marriage was given, both heard the low, sad wail above their heads. The young man deserted her, she died of a broken heart, and the night before her death, the Banshee's song, loud and clear, was heard outside the window of her mother's cottage. One of the O'Flahertys, of Galway, marched out of his castle with his men on a foray, and, as his troops filed through the gateway, the Banshee was heard high above the towers of the fortress. The next night she sang again, and was heard no more for a month, when his wife heard the wail under her window, and on the following day his followers brought back his corpse. One of the O'Neills of Shane Castle, in Antrim, heard the Banshee as he started on a journey before daybreak, and was accidentally killed some time after, but while on the same journey.

The wail most frequently comes at night, although cases are cited of Banshees singing during the daytime, and the song is often inaudible to all save the one for whom the warning is intended. This, however, is not general, the death notice being for the family rather than for the doomed individual. The spirit is generally alone, though rarely several are heard singing in chorus. A lady of the O'Flaherty family, greatly beloved for her social qualities, benevolence, and piety, was, some years ago, taken ill at the family mansion near Galway, though no uneasiness was felt on her account, as her ailment seemed nothing more than a slight cold. After she had remained in-doors for a day or two several of her acquaintances came to her room to enliven her imprisonment, and while the little party were merrily chatting, strange sounds were heard and all trembled and turned pale as they recognized the singing of a chorus of Banshees. The lady's ailment developed into pleurisy, and she died in a few days, the chorus being again heard in a sweet, plaintive requiem as the spirit was leaving her body. The honor of being warned by more than one Banshee is, however, very great, and comes only to the purest of the pure.

The "hateful Banshee" is much dreaded by members of a family against which she has enmity. A noble Irish family, whose name is still familiar in Mayo, is attended by a Banshee of this description. This Banshee is the spirit of a young girl deceived and afterwards murdered by a former head of the family. With her dying breath she cursed her murderer, and promised she would attend him and his forever. Many years passed, the chieftain reformed his ways, and his youthful crime was almost forgotten even by himself, when, one night, he and his family were seated by the fire, and suddenly the most horrid shrieks were heard outside the castle walls. All ran out, but saw nothing. During the night the screams continued as though the castle were besieged by demons, and the unhappy man recognized, in the cry of the Banshee, the voice of the young girl he had murdered. The next night he was assassinated by one of his followers, when again the wild, unearthly screams of the spirit were heard, exulting over his fate. Since that night, the "hateful Banshee" has never failed to notify the family, with shrill cries of revengeful gladness, when the time of one of their number had arrived.

Banshees are not often seen, but those that have made themselves visible differ as much in personal appearance as in the character of their cries. The "friendly Banshee" is a young and beautiful female spirit, with pale face, regular, well-formed features, hair sometimes coal-black, sometimes golden; eyes blue, brown, or black. Her long, white drapery falls below her feet as she floats in the air, chanting her weird warning, lifting her hands as if in pitying tenderness bestowing a benediction on the soul she summons to the invisible world. The "hateful Banshee" is a horrible hag, with angry, distorted features; maledictions are written in every line of her wrinkled face, and her outstretched arms call down curses on the doomed member of the hated race. Though generally the only intimation of the presence of the Banshee is her cry, a notable instance of the contrary exists in the family of the O'Reardons, to the doomed member of which the Banshee always appears in the shape of an exceedingly beautiful woman, who

> *The honor of being warned by more than one Banshee is, however, very great, and comes only to the purest of the pure.*

sings a song so sweetly solemn as to reconcile him to his approaching fate.

The prophetic spirit does not follow members of a family who go to a foreign land, but should death overtake them abroad, she gives notice of the misfortune to those at home. When the Duke of Wellington died, the Banshee was heard wailing round the house of his ancestors, and during the Napoleonic campaigns, she frequently notified Irish families of the death in battle of Irish officers and soldiers. The night before the battle of the Boyne several Banshees were heard singing in the air over the Irish camp, the truth of their prophecy being verified by the death-roll of the next day.

How the Banshee is able to obtain early and accurate information from foreign parts of the death in battle of Irish soldiers is yet undecided in Hibernian mystical circles. Some believe that there are, in addition to the two kinds already mentioned, "silent Banshees," who act as attendants to the members of old families, one to each member; that these silent spirits follow and observe, bringing back intelligence to the family Banshee at home, who then, at the proper seasons, sings her dolorous strain. A partial confirmation of this theory is seen in the fact that the Banshee has given notice at the family seat in Ireland of deaths in battles fought in every part of the world. From North America, the West Indies, Africa, Australia, India, China; from every point to which Irish regiments have followed the roll of the British drums, news of the prospective shedding of Irish blood has been brought home, and the slaughter preceded by a Banshee wail outside the ancestral windows. But it is due to the reader to state, that this silent Banshee theory is by no means well or generally received, the burden of evidence going to show that there are only two kinds of Banshees, and that, in a supernatural way, they know the immediate future of those in whom they are interested, not being obliged to leave Ireland for the purpose of obtaining their information.

Such is the wild Banshee, once to be heard in every part of Ireland, and formerly believed in so devoutly that to express a doubt of her existence was little less than blasphemy. Now, however, as she attends only the old families and does not change to the new, with the disappearance of many noble Irish names during the last half century have gone also their Banshees, until in only a few retired districts of the west coast is the dreaded spirit still found, while in most parts of the island she has become only a superstition, and from the majesty of a death-boding angel, is rapidly sinking to a level with the Fairy, the Leprechawn and the Pooka; the subject for tales to amuse the idle and terrify the young.

3

GHOSTLY TALES
OF THE BANSHEE

*Every difficulty slurred over will be a ghost to disturb
your repose later on.*

—Chopin

Joseph Thomas Sheridan Le Fanu, Irish writer of Gothic
tales and mystery novels, was a key author in the ghost story genre in the 19th century. Born in Dublin in 1814, he's
known for writing *Uncle Silas, Carmilla,* and *The House by
the Churchyard.* Despite his literary successes, his personal
life was somewhat troubled, as his wife suffered from intense
neurotic symptoms. She experienced anxiety after several
relatives died, and in April 1858, she suffered a "hysterical
attack" that led to her death the following day. Le Fanu ex-
presses anguish in his diaries, suggesting he felt guilt as well

as grief in the aftermath of her demise. He refused to write fiction until his mother died in 1861.

> *Carmilla*, Le Fanu's 1872 novella, is now considered the first example of stories about female and lesbian vampires. In the story, Carmilla gets chased and beheaded by the townspeople after they discover she's a vampire.

THE BANSHEE
by J.S. Le Fanu

So old a Munster family as the Bailys, of Lough Guir, could not fail to have their attendant banshee. Everyone attached to the family knew this well, and could cite evidences of that unearthly distinction. I heard Miss Baily relate the only experience she had personally had of that wild spiritual sympathy.

She said that, being then young, she and Miss Susan undertook a long attendance upon the sick bed of their sister, Miss Kitty, whom I have heard remembered among her contemporaries as the merriest and most entertaining of human beings. This light-hearted young lady was dying of consumption. The sad duties of such attendance being divided among many sisters, as there then were, the night watches devolved upon the two ladies I have named: I think, as being the eldest.

It is not improbable that these long and melancholy vigils, lowering the spirits and exciting the nervous system, prepared them for illusions. At all events, one night at dead of night, Miss Baily and her sister, sitting in the dying lady's room, heard such sweet and melancholy music as they had never heard before. It seemed to them like distant cathedral music. The room of the dying girl had its windows toward the yard, and the old castle stood near, and full in sight. The music was not in the house, but seemed to come from the yard, or beyond it. Miss Anne Baily took a candle, and went down the back stairs. She opened the back door, and, standing there, heard the same faint but solemn harmony, and could not tell whether it most resembled the distant music of instruments, or a choir of voices. It seemed to come through the windows of the old castle, high in the air. But when she approached the tower, the music, she thought, came from above the house, at the other side of the yard; and thus perplexed, and at last frightened, she returned.

This aerial music both she and her sister, Miss Susan Baily, avowed that they distinctly heard, and for a long time. Of the fact she was clear, and she spoke of it with great awe.

4

LEGENDARY
LEGENDS

"Prophet!" said I, "thing of evil!—prophet still, if bird or devil!"

—EDGAR ALLAN POE, FROM "THE RAVEN"

Thomas Crofton Croker was an Irish antiquarian as well as a writer. He devoted his life to the collection of Irish poetry and folklore. His book on the south of Ireland went through six editions and was translated into German by the Brothers Grimm. Along with "Legends of the Banshee," he is well-known for his most famous merrow-themed story, "The Soul Cages."

Legends of the Banshee
by T. Crofton Croker

"Who sits upon the heath forlorn,
With robe so free and tresses torn?
Anon she pours a harrowing strain,
And then—she sits all mute again!
Now peals the wild funereal cry—
And now—it sinks into a sigh."

—Ourawns

The Reverend Charles Bunworth was rector of Buttevant, in the county of Cork, about the middle of the last century. He was a man of unaffected piety, and of sound learning; pure in heart, and benevolent in intention. By the rich he was respected, and by the poor beloved; nor did a difference of creed prevent their looking up to "the minister" (so was Mr. Bunworth called by them) in matters of difficulty and in seasons of distress, confident of receiving from him the advice and assistance that a father would afford to his children. He was the friend and the benefactor of the surrounding country—to him, from the neighbouring town of Newmarket, came both Curran and Yelverton for advice and instruction, previous to their entrance at Dublin College. Young, indigent and inexperienced, these afterwards eminent men received from him, in addition to the advice they sought, pecuniary aid; and the brilliant career which was theirs, justified the discrimination of the giver.

But what extended the fame of Mr. Bunworth, far beyond the limits of the parishes adjacent to his own, was his performance on the Irish harp, and his hospitable reception and entertainment of the poor harpers who travelled from house to house about the country. Grateful to their patron, these itinerant minstrels sang his praises to the tingling accompaniment of their harps, invoking in return for his bounty abundant blessings on his white head, and celebrating in their rude verses the blooming charms of his daughters, Elizabeth and Mary. It was all these poor fellows could do; but who can doubt that their gratitude was sincere, when, at the time of Mr. Bunworth's death, no less than fifteen harps were deposited in the loft of his granary, bequeathed to him by the last members of a race which has now ceased to exist. Trifling, no doubt, in intrinsic value were these relics, yet there is something in gifts of the heart that merits preservation; and it is to be regretted that, when he died, these harps were broken up one after the other, and used as fire-wood by an ignorant follower of the family, who, on a removal to Cork for a temporary change of scene, was left in charge of the house.

The circumstances attending the death of Mr. Bunworth may be doubted by some; but there are still living credible witnesses who declare their authenticity, and who can be produced to attest most, if not all of the following particulars.

About a week previous to his dissolution, and early in the evening a noise was heard at the hall-door resembling the shearing of sheep; but at the time no particular attention was paid to it. It was nearly eleven o'clock the same night, when Kavanagh, the herdsman, returned from Mallow, whither he had been sent in the afternoon for some medicine, and was observed by Miss Bunworth, to whom he delivered the parcel, to be much agitated. At this time, it must be observed, her father was by no means considered in danger.

"What is the matter, Kavanagh?" asked Miss Bunworth: but the poor fellow, with a bewildered look, only uttered, "The master, Miss—the master—he is going from us;" and, overcome with real grief, he burst into a flood of tears.

Miss Bunworth, who was a woman of strong nerve, inquired if any thing he had learned in Mallow induced him to suppose that her father was worse. "No, Miss," said Kavanagh; "it was not in Mallow—"

"Kavanagh," said Miss Bunworth, with that stateliness of manner for which she is said to have been remarkable, "I fear you have been drinking, which, I must say, I did not expect at such a time as the present, when it was your duty to have kept yourself sober—I thought you might have been trusted—what should we have done if you had broken the medicine bottle, or lost it? For the doctor said it was of the greatest consequence that your master should take the medicine to-night. But I will speak to you in the morning, when you are in a fitter state to understand what I say."

Kavanagh looked up with a stupidity of aspect which did not serve to remove the impression of his being drunk, as his eyes appeared heavy and dull after the flood of tears—but his voice was not that of an intoxicated person.

"Miss," said he, "as I hope to receive mercy hereafter, neither bit nor sup has passed my lips since I left this house; but the master—"

"Speak softly," said Miss Bunworth; "he sleeps, and is going on as well as we could expect."

"Praise be to God for that, any way," replied Kavanagh; "but oh! Miss, he is going from us surely—we will lose him—the master—we will lose him, we will lose him!" and he wrung his hands together.

"What is it you mean, Kavanagh?" asked Miss Bunworth.

"Is it mean?" said Kavanagh: "the Banshee has come for him, Miss, and 'tis not I alone who have heard her."

"'Tis an idle superstition," said Miss Bunworth.

"May be so," replied Kavanagh, as if the words 'idle superstition' only sounded upon his ear without reaching his mind—"May be so," he continued; "but as I came through the glen of Ballybeg, she was along with me, keening, and screeching, and clapping her hands, by my side, every step of the way, with her long white hair falling about her shoulders, and I could hear her repeat the master's name every now and then, as plain as ever I heard it. When I came to the old abbey, she parted from me there, and turned into the pigeon-field next the berrin ground, and folding her cloak about her, down she sat under the tree that was struck by the lightning, and began keening so bitterly, that it went through one's heart to hear it."

> *Down she sat under the tree that was struck by the lightning, and began keening so bitterly, that it went through one's heart to hear it.*

Banshee, correctly written she-fairies or women fairies, credulously supposed, by the common people, to be so affected to certain families, that they are heard to sing mournful lamentations about their houses at night, whenever any of the family labours under a sickness which is to end in death. But no families which are not of an ancient and noble stock are believed to be honoured with this fairy privilege.

—*O'Brien's Irish Dictionary*

"Kavanagh," said Miss Bunworth, who had, however, listened attentively to this remarkable relation, "my father is, I believe, better; and I hope will himself soon be up and able to convince you that all this is but your own fancy; nevertheless, I charge you not to mention what you have told me, for there is no occasion to frighten your fellow-servants with the story."

Mr. Bunworth gradually declined; but nothing particular occurred until the night previous to his death: that night both his daughters, exhausted with continued attendance and watching, were prevailed upon to seek some repose; and an elderly lady, a near relative and friend of the family, remained by the bedside of their father. The old gentleman then lay in the parlour, where he had been in the morning removed at his own request, fancying the change would afford him relief; and the head of his bed was placed close to the window. In a room adjoining sat some male friends, and, as usual on like occasions of illness, in the kitchen many of the followers of the family had assembled.

The night was serene and moonlit—the sick man slept—and nothing broke the stillness of their melancholy watch, when the little party in the room adjoining the parlour, the door of which stood open, was suddenly roused by a sound at the window near the bed: a rose tree grew outside the window, so close as to touch the glass; this was forced aside with some noise, and a low moaning was heard, accompanied by clapping of hands, as if of a female in deep affliction. It seemed as if the sound proceeded from a person holding her mouth close to the window. The lady who sat by the bedside of Mr. Bunworth went into the adjoining room, and in a tone of alarm, inquired of the gentlemen there, if they had heard the Banshee? Skeptical of supernatural appearances, two of them rose hastily and went out to discover the cause of these sounds, which they also had distinctly heard. They walked all around the house, examining every spot of ground, particularly near the window from whence the voice had proceeded; the bed of earth beneath, in which the rose tree was planted, had been recently dug, and the print of a footstep—if the tree had been forced aside by mortal hand— would have inevitably remained; but they could perceive no such impression; and an unbroken stillness reigned without. Hoping to dispel the mystery, they continued their search anxiously along the road, from the straightness of which and the lightness of the night, they were enabled to see some distance around them; but all was silent and deserted, and they returned surprised and disappointed. How much more then were they astonished at learning that the whole time of their absence, those who remained within the house had heard the moaning and clapping of hands even louder and more distinct than before they had gone out; and no sooner was the door of the room closed on them, than they again heard the same mournful sounds! Every succeeding hour the sick man became worse, and as the first glimpse of the morning appeared, Mr. Bunworth expired.

5

THE BANSHEE
ACCORDING TO YEATS

Fifteen apparitions have I seen;
The worst a coat upon a coat-hanger.

—William Butler Yeats, from
"The Apparitions"

William Butler Yeats (1865–1939) is often regarded as one of the most prized Irish poets and was awarded the Nobel Prize for Literature in 1923. It is no secret that Yeats had a penchant for ghosts, folklore, and the occult from a young age, and these themes influenced his writing, particularly in the latter years. In 1911 he joined one of the first official paranormal investigation organizations, known as "The Ghost Club," whose early members included Charles Dickens and later members included Sir Arthur Conan Doyle and Algernon Blackwood.

In the following excerpt from his greater work *Fairy and Folk Tales of the Irish Peasantry*, Yeats describes the typical Irish banshee and traditions that surround it, including the connection between keening—the Irish wale of mourning—and the howl of the banshee. The description of the banshee coach, which is manned by a headless horseman (a Dullahan) driving headless horses is enough to make you more than just hurry home along the path as the darkness creeps in. You might find yourself in an all-out sprint. Still, running won't do you any good. The banshee is simply rolling out the red carpet for the grand entrance of death itself. And no one escapes that.

The Banshee

by W.B. Yeats

The *banshee* (from *ban* [*bean*], a woman, and *shee* [*sidhe*], a fairy) is an attendant fairy that follows the old families, and none but them, and wails before a death. Many have seen her as she goes wailing and clapping her hands. The keen [*caoine*], the funeral cry of the peasantry, is said to be an imitation of her cry. When more than one banshee is present, and they wail and sing in chorus, it is for the death of some holy or great one.

An omen that sometimes accompanies the banshee is the *coach-a-bower* [*cóiste-bodhar*]—an immense black coach, mounted by a coffin, and drawn by headless horses driven by a Dullahan. It will go rumbling to your door, and if you open it, according to Croker, a basin of blood will be thrown in your face.

These headless phantoms are found elsewhere than in Ireland. In 1807 two of the sentries stationed outside St. James's Park died of fright. A headless woman, the upper part of her body naked, used to pass at midnight, and scale the railings. After a time the sentries were stationed no longer at the haunted spot.

In Norway the heads of corpses were cut off to make their ghosts feeble. Thus came into existence the Dullahans, perhaps; unless indeed, they are descended from that Irish giant who swam across the Channel with his head in his teeth.

6

IS THAT A BANSHEE OR ARE YOU JUST HAPPY TO SEE ME?

There is nothing impossible in the existence of the super-natural: its existence seems to me decidedly probable.

—GEORGE SANTAYANA, FROM
THE GENTEEL TRADITION AT BAY

Banshees, while technically unique to Ireland, are known by many other names in other countries. Their international counterparts include the German Lady in White, the misleadingly sweet singing phantasm of Italy, family ghosts, hags, witches, woeful bridal phantoms, and many, many other terrifying creatures that haunt the globe. O'Donnell writes about this in the following "Alleged Counterparts of the Banshee."

Alleged Counterparts of the Banshee

by Elliott O'Donnell

No country besides Ireland possesses a Banshee, though some countries possess a family or national ghost somewhat resembling it. In Germany, for example, popular tradition is full of rumours of white ladies who haunt castles, woods, rivers, and mountains, where they may be seen combing their yellow hair, or playing on harps or spinning. They usually, as their name would suggest, wear white dresses, and not infrequently yellow or green shoes of a most dainty and artistic design. Sometimes they are sad, sometimes gay; sometimes they warn people of approaching death or disaster, and sometimes, by their beauty, they blind men to an impending peril, and thus lure them on to their death. When beautiful, they are often very beautiful, though nearly always of the same type—golden hair and long blue eyes; they are rarely dark, and their hair is never of that peculiar copper and golden hue that is so common among Banshees. When ugly, they are generally ugly indeed—either repulsive old crones, not unlike the witches in Grimm's Fairy Tales, or death-heads mockingly arrayed in the paraphernalia of the young; but their ugliness does not seem to embrace that ghastly satanic mockery, that diabolical malevolence that is inseparable from the malignant form of Banshee, and which inspires in the beholders such a peculiar and unparalleled horror.

Occasionally, too, the German family ghost, like the Banshee, is heard playing on a harp, but here I think the likeness ends. There are no very striking characteristics in the appearance of the White Lady of the Hohenzollerns, she would seem to be neither very beautiful nor the reverse; nor does she convey the impression of belonging to any very remote age; on the contrary, she might well be the earth-bound spirit of someone who died in the Middle Ages or even later.

In December, 1628, she was seen in the Royal Palace in Berlin, and was heard to say, *"Veni, judica vivos et mortuos; judicum mihi adhuc superest"*—that is to say, "Come judge the quick and the dead—I wait for judgment." She also manifested herself to one of the Fredericks of Prussia, who regarded her advent as a sure sign of his approaching death, which it was, for he died shortly afterwards. We next read of her appearing in Bohemia at the Castle of Neuhaus. One of the princesses of the royal house was trying on a new head-gear before a mirror, and, thinking her waiting-maid was near at hand, she inquired of her the time. To the Princess's horror, however, instead of the maid answering her, a strange figure all in white, which her instincts told her was the famous national ghost, stepped out from behind a screen and exclaimed, *"Zehn uhr ist es irh Liebden!"* "It is ten o'clock, your love"; the last two words being the mode of address usually adopted in Germany and Austria by Royalties when speaking to one another. The Princess was soon afterwards taken ill and died.

A faithful account of the appearance of the White Lady was published in *The Iris* a Frankfort journal, in 1829, and was vouched for by the editor, George Doring. Doring's mother, who was companion to one of the ladies at the Prussian Court, had two daughters, aged fourteen and fifteen, who were in the habit of visiting her at the Palace. On one occasion, when the two girls were alone in their mother's sitting-room, doing some needlework, they were immeasurably surprised to hear the sounds of music, proceeding, so it seemed to them, from behind a big stove that occupied one corner of the apartment. One girl got up, and, taking a yard measure, struck the spot where she fancied the music was coming from; whereupon the measure was instantly snatched from her hand, the music, at the same time, ceasing. She was so badly frightened that she ran out of the room and took refuge in someone else's apartment.

On her return some minutes later, she found her sister lying on the floor in a dead faint. On coming to, this sister stated that directly the other had quitted the apartment, the music had begun again and, not only that, but the figure of a woman, all in white, had suddenly risen from behind the stove and began to advance towards her, causing her instantly to faint with fright.

The lady in whose house the occurrence took place, on being acquainted with what had happened, had the flooring near the stove taken up; but, instead of discovering the treasure which she had hoped might be there, a quantity of quick-lime only was found; and the affair eventually getting to the King's ears, he displayed no surprise, but merely expressed his belief that the apparition the girl had seen was that of the Countess Agnes of Orlamunde, who had been bricked up alive in that room.

She had been the mistress of a former Margrave of Brandenburg, by whom she had had two children, and when the Margrave's legitimate wife died the Countess hoped he would marry her. This, however, he declined to do on the plea that her offspring, at his death, would very probably dispute the heirship to the property with the children of his lawful marriage. The Countess then, in order to remove this obstacle to her union, poisoned her two children, which act so disgusted the Margrave that he had her walled up alive in the room where she had committed the crimes. The King went on to explain that the phantasm appeared about every seven years, but more often to children, to whom it was believed to be very much attached, than to adults.

William Brereton in his "Travels" gives rather a different description of this ghost. He says that the Queen of Bohemia told him "that at Berlin—the Elector of Brandenberg's house—before the death of anyone related in blood to that house, there appears and walks up and down that house like unto a ghost in a white sheet, which walks during the time of their sickness until their death."

In this account it will be noticed that there is no mention of sex, so that the reader can only speculate as to whether the apparition was the ghost of a man or a woman. Its appearance, however, according to this account, strongly suggests a ghost of the sepulchral and death-head type—an ordinary species of elemental—which suggestion is not apparent in any other description of it that we have hitherto come across. Other ancient German and Austrian families, besides those of the ruling houses, possess their family ghosts, and here again, as in the parallel case of the Irish and their Banshee, the family ghost of the Germans or Austrians is by no means confined to the "White Lady." In some cases of German family haunting, for example, the phenomenon is a roaring lion, in others a howling dog; and in others a bell or gong, or sepulchral toned clock striking at some unusual hour, and generally thirteen times. In all instances, however, no matter whether the family ghost be German, Irish, or Austrian, the purpose of its manifestations is the same—to predict death or some very grave calamity.

> *No matter whether the family ghost be German, Irish, or Austrian, the purpose of its manifestations is the same—to predict death or some very grave calamity.*

In Italy there are several families of distinction possessing a family ghost that somewhat resembles the Banshee. According to Cardau and Henningius Grosius the ancient Venetian family of Donati possess a ghost in the form of a man's head, which is seen looking through a doorway whenever any member of the family is doomed to die. The following extract from their joint work serves as an illustration of it:

"Jacopo Donati, one of the most important families in Venice, had a child, the heir to the family, very ill. At night, when in bed, Donati saw the door of his chamber opened and the head of a man thrust in. Knowing that it was not one of his servants, he roused the house, drew his sword, went over the whole palace, all the servants declaring that they had seen such a head thrust in at the doors of their several chambers at the same hour; the fastenings were found all secure, so that no one could have come in from without. The next day the child died."

Other families in Italy, a branch of the Paoli, for example, is haunted by very sweet music, the voice of a woman singing to the accompaniment of a harp or guitar, and invariably before a death.

Of the family ghost in Spain I have been able to gather but little information. There, too, some of the oldest families seem to possess ghosts that follow the fortunes, both at home and abroad, of the families to which they are attached, but with the exception of this one point of resemblance there seems to be in them little similarity to the Banshee.

In Denmark and Sweden the likeness between the family ghost and the Banshee is decidedly pronounced. Quite a number of old Scandinavian families possess attendant spirits very much after the style of the Banshee; some very beautiful and sympathetic, and some quite the reverse; the most notable difference being that in the Scandinavian apparition there is none of that ghastly mixture of the grave, antiquity, and hell that is so characteristic of the baleful type of Banshee, and which would seem to distinguish it from the ghosts  of all other countries. The beautiful Scandinavian phantasms more closely resemble fairies or angels than any women of this earth, whilst the hideous ones have all the grotesqueness and crude horror of the witches of Andersen or Grimm. There is nothing about them, as there so often is in the Banshee, to make one wonder if they can be the phantasms of any long extinct race, or people, for example, that might have hailed from the missing continent of Atlantis, or have been in Ireland prior to the coming of the Celts.

The Scandinavian family ghosts are frankly either elementals or the earth-bound spirits of the much more recent dead. Yet, as I have said, they have certain points in common with the Banshee. They prognosticate death or disaster; they scream and wail like women in the throes of some great mental or physical agony; they sob or laugh; they occasionally tap on the window-panes, or play on the harp; they sometimes haunt in pairs, a kind spirit and an evilly disposed one attending the fortunes of the same family; and they keep exclusively to the very oldest families. Oddly enough at times the Finnish family ghost assumes the guise of a man. Burton, for example, in his "Anatomy of Melancholy," tells us "that near Rufus Nova, in Finland, there is a lake in which, when the governor of the castle dies, a spectrum is seen in the habit of Orion, with a harp, and makes excellent music, like those clocks in Cheshire which (they say) presage death to the masters of the family; or that oak in Lanthadran Park in Cornwall, which foreshadows so much."

Beginning with Scotland, Sir Walter Scott was strong in his belief in the Banshee, which he described as one of the most beautiful superstitions of Europe. In his "Letters on Demonology" he says: "Several families of the Highlands of Scotland anciently laid claim to the distinction of an attendant spirit, who performed the office of the Irish Banshee," and he particularly referred to the ghostly cries and lamentations which foreboded death to members of the Clan of MacLean of Lochbery. But though many of the Highland families do possess such a ghost, unlike the Banshee, it is not restricted to the feminine sex, nor does its origin, as a rule, date back to anything like such remote times. It would seem, indeed, to belong to a much more ordinary species of phantasm, a species which is seldom accompanied by music or any other sound, and which by no means always prognosticates death, although on many occasions it has done so.

Mr. Ingram, in his "Haunted Houses and Family Legends," quotes several well authenticated instances of manifestations by this apparition, the last occurring, according to him, in the year 1899, though I have heard from other reliable sources that it has been heard at a much more recent date. The origin of this haunting is generally thought to be comparatively modern, and not to date further back than two or three hundred years, if as far, which, of course, puts it on quite a different category from that of the Banshee, though its mission is, without doubt, the same. According to Mr. Ingram, a former Lord Airlie, becoming jealous of one of his retainers or emissaries who was a drummer, had him thrust in his drum and hurled from a top window of the castle into the courtyard beneath, where he was dashed to pieces. With his dying breath the drummer cursed not only Lord Airlie, but his descendants, too, and ever since that event his apparition has persistently haunted the family.

Other Highland families that possess special ghosts are a branch of the Macdonnells, that have a phantom piper, whose mournful piping invariably means that some member or other of the clan is shortly doomed to die; and the Stanleys who have a female apparition that signalises her advent by shrieking, weeping, and moaning before the death of any of the family. Perhaps of all Scottish ghosts this last one most closely resembles the Banshee, though there are distinct differences, chiefly with regard to the appearance of the phantoms—the Scottish one differing essentially in her looks and attire from the Irish ghost—and their respective origins, that of the Stanley apparition being, in all probability, of much later date than the Banshee.

There are other old Scottish family ghosts, all very distinct from the Banshee, though a few bear some slight resemblance to it, but as my space is restricted, I will pass on to family ghosts of a more or less similar type that are to be met with in England.

To begin with, the Oxenhams of Devonshire the heiress of Sir James Oxenham, and the bride that is invariably seen before the death of any member of the family. According to a well-known Devonshire ballad, a bird answering to this description flew over the guests at the wedding of the heiress of Sir James Oxenham, and the bride was killed the following day by a suitor she had unceremoniously jilted.

The Arundels of Wardour have a ghost in the form of two white owls, it being alleged that whenever two birds of this species are seen perched on the house where any of this family are living, some one member of them is doomed to die very shortly.

Equally famous is the ghost of the Cliftons of Nottinghamshire, which takes the shape of a sturgeon that is seen swimming in the river Trent, opposite Clifton Hall, the chief seat of the family, whenever one of the Cliftons is on the eve of dying.

Then, again, there is the white hand of the Squires of Worcestershire, a family that is now practically extinct. According to local tradition this family was for many generations haunted by the very beautiful hand of a woman, that was always seen protruding through the wall of the room containing that member of the family who was fated to die soon. Most ghost hands are said to be grey and filmy, but this one, according to some eye-witnesses, appears to have borne an extraordinary resemblance to that of a living person. It was slender and perfectly proportioned, with very tapering fingers and very long and beautifully kept filbert nails—the sort of hand one sees in portraits of women of bygone ages, but which one very rarely meets with in the present generation.

Other families that possess ghosts are the Yorkshire Middletons, who are always apprised of the death of one of their members by the appearance of a nun; and the Byrons of Newstead Abbey, who, according to the great poet of that name, were haunted by a black Friar that used to be seen wandering about the cloisters and other parts of the monasterial building before the death of any member of the family.

> *According to local tradition this family was for many generations haunted by the very beautiful hand of a woman, that was always seen protruding through the wall of the room containing that member of the family who was fated to die soon.*

In England, there seems to be quite a number of White Lady phantoms, most of them, however, haunting houses and not families, and none of them bearing any resemblance to the Banshee. Indeed, there is a far greater dissimilarity between the English and Irish types of family ghosts than there is between the Irish and those of any of the nations I have hitherto discussed.

7

BANSHEE BANTER

I bet the worst part about dying is the part where your whole life passes before you.

—JANE WAGNER

I know you want to believe that this entire section on banshees has been dedicated to a fictional creature that is brought on by my grief or heavy drinking. I wish I could assure you that this were the case, but alas, banshees are as real as the lock on the door you should go right now and bolt. Not that a bit of steel and wood will keep out a wild banshee. Still, it is very likely that in your lifetime you will not encounter a banshee, and for this you can rest a tiny bit easier. Here are a few random tidbits of banshee banter that I hope will lighten the mood, since you should now be properly scared.

Banshee, Pennsylvania

The creator of *True Blood* has a new show, *Banshee*, which focuses on Antony Starr as Lucas Hood, an ex-con and master thief masquerading as the sheriff of the small town of Banshee, Pennsylvania. Though not about the mythological ghostly and ghastly banshees themselves, the title presumably comes from the lead character's "handsome face" of trickery that lures victims in. He is their charming, enchanting harbinger of death.

A Cemetery Rose

A gardener's delight, the High Country Banshee Rose is an heirloom, damask rose that blooms prolific, blushing pink flowers. It belongs to a group of roses known among horticulturalists as Fairmount Cemetery Roses, having been discovered thriving in Denver's historic Fairmount Cemetery.

Screaming Banshee

If you'd like to get in the mood to get wild with your own creatures of the night, whip up a Screaming Banshee with equal parts (1 oz.) vodka and banana liqueur; ½ oz. each of crème de cacao and cream. Shake with ice and serve in a chilled martini glass. I like mine with a shot of whipped cream on top!

Should you find yourself in Chico, California, you can stop in at the Banshee, a local pub that serves food, drinks, and presumably, a screaming good time.

CRY, CRY BABY

The American counterpart to the banshee dates back to the 18th century, though American banshees primarily appear as ghosts and not necessarily as harbingers of impending death or misfortune. They are most often sighted or heard near rivers and streams, where many believe they are mourning drowned children.

These stories may also relate to the Crybaby Bridges of Ohio. Ohio has an inordinate amount of what are known as crybaby bridges—bridges that have had live babies thrown over them.

The circumstances behind each incident are pretty much the same: a young woman has been able to hide her pregnancy, but when her child is born, she throws it over a bridge to fend for itself in the murky deep. It is said that if you turn off your car engine on one of Ohio's crybaby bridges, you can hear the wails of a newborn child in the wind.

FALSE BANSHEE

In *The Dead Files: A Banshee's Cry*, a recent episode of the Travel Channel's popular show, hosts Steve and Amy investigate a haunted bar in upstate New York known as Smalley's Inn. Based on her own impressions, as well as descriptions of the ghost's aggressive behavior toward the proprietor and employees, Amy believes the ghost to be a banshee. As she describes it, a banshee in Ireland or Scotland wanders the countryside, wailing and moaning, and it is said if you see one, your own death is imminent. If you hear one, it will be the death of someone close to you. When a photograph is produced of the original innkeeper's first wife, Amy breathes a sigh of relief upon recognizing the ghost she has seen and the others have described. Because banshees are of the fae or supernatural realm, a living person cannot become a banshee, and the ghost they've all been seeing is that of the long-dead wife, projecting herself as a banshee in order to prevent an exorcism. You'll have to watch the whole episode to find out what happens—it's a spine-tingling show!

Star Wars fans may recall the Corellian banshee bird, a bird native to the planet of Corellia known for its loud screams.

Part Two

WEREWOLVES

To him who is in fear everything rustles.

—SOPHOCLES

WHAT BIG EYES YOU HAVE

Werewolves are an interesting pack. Not quite as sexy as vampires and not as revered as witches, they are typically viewed with a mix of sympathy and disdain—*Teen Wolf* being the exception. The werewolf appears to be older and more universal in culture than vampires or other supernatural creatures. Though many of us think of werewolves as the classic woodland man-turned-wolf, there are many cross-cultural variants of werewolves, often referred to as shape-shifters. In legends we find the Chinese *P'an Hu*, the *Wendigo* of Algonquian peoples, and the Cajun *Rougarou* or *Roux-Ga-Roux*. Our literary past is littered with werewolves, most famously the Big Bad Wolf himself, who lurks in the forest and lusts after Little Red Riding Hood. In 1933, Guy Endore wrote one of the single most important contributions to werewolf literature, *The Werewolf of Paris*. I like to think of him sifting through old werewolf stories like "The Werewolf," written by Eugene Field in the 19th century, drawing inspiration on the folklore of those lycanthropy enthusiasts who came before him. Of note, this novel later became the 1960s feature film of freakery, *The Curse of the Werewolf*.

Speaking of the big screen, the aforementioned *Teen Wolf* is certainly an iconic symbol of lycanthropic fun, but perhaps more iconic still is *The Wolf Man*, played by the great Lon Chaney. This movie also stars one of my beyond-the-grave crushes Bela Lugosi, who actually plays the werewolf that infects Chaney. I mean, could it get any dreamier? Actually, it does, in *Frankenstein vs. the Wolfman*, which stars Bela Lugosi as Frankenstein's monster and Lon Chaney again as the Wolfman. But I digress. (Check out my bucket list of werewolf flicks at the end of the book.)

We fear the mindless zombie, the ancient mummy, or even the licentious vampire, but we don't fear the werewolf so much as we feel sorry for it. It is a wild beast caught in a trap. We worry for the werewolf; we wish its life could be another way. We don't want to become werewolves the way we want super powers or immortality. We want the werewolf to be free of the curse that binds it. Free to be either beast or man, not tragically stuck being both.

Here are a few interesting facts about werewolves you may not know:

- Werewolves are not always mean. In medieval romances, such as the French poem *Guillaume de Pal-erme,* the werewolf is not the terrifying creature of more modern tales but is rather benign, appearing more like a victim and less like the enemy.

- Werewolves are not always male. The 1588 story from the mountains of Auvergne tells the tale of a she-wolf whose paw was cut off by a hunter. When he opened the bag in which he had placed his prized paw, he discovered instead a woman's hand. It didn't take long to figure out who was missing the hand (a nobleman's wife) and she was burnt at the stake. That's one way to end a marriage . . .

- Werewolves are not always wolves. Were-creatures can be in the form of many beasts. In variations of lore from around the world, we find examples of were-cats, were-sharks, were-bears, and even a were-dolphin.

• Werewolves are not always fictional. There is a rare but very real disease now called clinical lycanthropy. Those diagnosed believe themselves to be able to transform into a non-human animal, specifically a wolf.

Those of you who aren't such fans of the werewolf will want to avoid the darkest woods at night, especially any woods that look much like those described in the following story—full of ravens, vampires, and serpents—and you should never, ever go out on a full moon. You may fare well, as the heroine of our story does, but to hedge your bets you might want to keep a little satchel with you full of silver bullets (you'll need a gun to fire them), or a silver dagger if you can't get a gun. If you are a dead-mark, a bow and arrow might do, but it is very risky. Oh, and make sure to stock up on wolfsbane. It will ward off wolves, but it can also be an antidote to wolf bite if taken within a few hours of contact. I can't guarantee that these things will protect you, but they will at least give you something to do in your moment of panic, when your eyes

meet the glowing green eyes of your hirsute hellion, and you know that you are done for. After all, there are much, much less glamorous ways to die.

FILMY FACTS ABOUT
THE FURRY BEASTS

- One of the first films about werewolves is a silent French film called *Le Loup-Garou* that was released in 1923. The very first werewolf film, innocuously titled *The Werewolf*, has been lost since its release in 1913.

- *Werewolf of London* (1935) was the first film to feature anthropomorphic werewolves that walked on two legs.

- While many assume Michael Jackson turns into a werewolf in his music video for "Thriller," according to famous director John Landis, he actually more closely resembles a were-cat.

8

THE SWEETEST WOLF

The greatest happiness of life is the conviction that we are loved, loved for ourselves, or rather loved in spite of ourselves.

—Victor Hugo

Eugene Field was perhaps best known for his delightful stories, lullabies, and nursery rhymes for children. His work was so popular in its day that the great painter Maxfield Parrish illustrated several of the storybooks. But one of his lesser-known and far more sinister works is this short story, "The Werewolf." A tangled tale of love and viciousness, jealousy and curses, the author's command of the written word comes across heart-wrenchingly throughout. When I first read the description of the forest in the following passage, I had a vision of one of the most disturbing and beautiful places imaginable—a place you want to be just as much as you want to run screaming from it. (Of course, I love to scream . . .)

The Werewolf
by Eugene Field

In the reign of Egbert the Saxon there dwelt in Britain a maiden named Yseult, who was beloved of all, both for her goodness and for her beauty. But, though many a youth came wooing her, she loved Harold only, and to him she plighted her troth.

Among the other youth of whom Yseult was beloved was Alfred, and he was sore angered that Yseult showed favor to Harold, so that one day Alfred said to Harold: "Is it right that old Siegfried should come from his grave and have Yseult to wife?" Then added he, "Prithee, good sir, why do you turn so white when I speak your grandsire's name?"

Then Harold asked, "What know you of Siegfried that you taunt me? What memory of him should vex me now?"

"We know and we know," retorted Alfred. "There are some tales told us by our grandmas we have not forgot."

So ever after that Alfred's words and Alfred's bitter smile haunted Harold by day and night.

Harold's grandsire, Siegfried the Teuton, had been a man of cruel violence. The legend said that a curse rested upon him, and that at certain times he was possessed of an evil spirit that wreaked its fury on mankind. But Siegfried had been dead full many years, and there was naught to mind the world of him save the legend and a cunning-wrought spear which he had from Brunehilde, the witch. This spear was such a weapon that it never lost its brightness, nor had its point been blunted. It hung in Harold's chamber, and it was the marvel among weapons of that time.

Yseult knew that Alfred loved her, but she did not know of the bitter words which Alfred had spoken to Harold. Her love for Harold was perfect in its trust and gentleness. But Alfred had hit the truth: the curse of old Siegfried was upon Harold—slumbering a century, it had awakened in the blood of the grandson, and Harold knew the curse that was upon him, and it was this that seemed to stand between him and Yseult. But love is stronger than all else, and Harold loved.

Harold did not tell Yseult of the curse that was upon him, for he feared that she would not love him if she knew. Whensoever he felt the fire of the curse burning in his veins he would say to her, "To-morrow I hunt the wild boar in the uttermost forest," or, "Next week I go stag-stalking among the distant northern hills." Even so it was that he ever made good excuse for his absence, and Yseult thought no evil things, for she was trustful; ay, though he went many times away and was long gone, Yseult suspected no wrong. So none beheld Harold when the curse was upon him in its violence.

Alfred alone bethought himself of evil things. "'Tis passing strange," quoth he, "that ever and anon this gallant lover should quit our company and betake himself whither none knoweth. In sooth 't will be well to have an eye on old Siegfried's grandson."

Harold knew that Alfred watched him zealously, and he was tormented by a constant fear that Alfred would discover the curse that was on him; but what gave him greater anguish was the fear that mayhap at some moment when he was in Yseult's presence, the curse would seize upon him and cause him to do great evil unto her, whereby she would be destroyed or her love for him would be undone forever. So Harold lived in terror, feeling that his love was hopeless, yet knowing not how to combat it.

Now, it befell in those times that the country round about was ravaged of a werewolf, a creature that was feared by all men howe'er so valorous. This werewolf was by day a man, but by night a wolf given to ravage and to slaughter, and having a charmed life against which no human agency availed aught. Wheresoever he went he attacked and devoured mankind, spreading terror and desolation round about, and the dream-readers said that the earth would not be freed from the werewolf until some man offered himself a voluntary sacrifice to the monster's rage.

Now, although Harold was known far and wide as a mighty huntsman, he had never set forth to hunt the werewolf, and, strange enow, the werewolf never ravaged the domain while Harold was therein. Whereat Alfred marvelled much, and oftentimes he said: "Our Harold is a wondrous huntsman. Who is like unto him in stalking the timid doe and in crippling the fleeing boar? But how passing well doth he time his absence from the haunts of the werewolf. Such valor beseemeth our young Siegfried."

Which being brought to Harold his heart flamed with anger, but he made no answer, lest he should betray the truth he feared.

It happened so about that time that Yseult said to Harold, "Wilt thou go with me to-morrow even to the feast in the sacred grove?"

"That can I not do," answered Harold. "I am privily summoned hence to Normandy upon a mission of which I shall some time tell thee. And I pray thee, on thy love for me, go not to the feast in the sacred grove without me."

"What say'st thou?" cried Yseult. "Shall I not go to the feast of Ste. Ælfreda? My father would be sore displeased were I not there with the other maidens. 'T were greatest pity that I should despite his love thus."

"But do not, I beseech thee," Harold implored. "Go not to the feast of Ste. Ælfreda in the sacred grove! And thou would thus love me, go not—see, thou my life, on my two knees I ask it!"

"How pale thou art," said Yseult, "and trembling."

"Go not to the sacred grove upon the morrow night," he begged.

Yseult marvelled at his acts and at his speech. Then, for the first time, she thought him to be jealous—whereat she secretly rejoiced (being a woman).

"Ah," quoth she, "thou dost doubt my love," but when she saw a look of pain come on his face she added—as if she repented of the words she had spoken—"or dost thou fear the werewolf?"

Then Harold answered, fixing his eyes on hers, "Thou hast said it; it is the werewolf that I fear."

"Why dost thou look at me so strangely, Harold?" cried Yseult. "By the cruel light in thine eyes one might almost take thee to be the werewolf!"

"Come hither, sit beside me," said Harold tremblingly, "and I will tell thee why I fear to have thee go to the feast of Ste. Ælfreda to-morrow evening. Hear what I dreamed last night. I dreamed I was the were-wolf—do not shudder, dear love, for 't was only a dream.

"A grizzled old man stood at my bedside and strove to pluck my soul from my bosom.

"'What would'st thou?' I cried.

"'Thy soul is mine,' he said, 'thou shalt live out my curse. Give me thy soul—hold back thy hands— give me thy soul, I say.'

"'Thy curse shall not be upon me,' I cried. 'What have I done that thy curse should rest upon me? Thou shalt not have my soul.'

"'For my offence shalt thou suffer, and in my curse thou shalt endure hell—it is so decreed.'

"So spake the old man, and he strove with me, and he prevailed against me, and he plucked my soul from my bosom, and he said, 'Go, search and kill'—and—and lo, I was a wolf upon the moor.

"The dry grass crackled beneath my tread. The darkness of the night was heavy and it oppressed me. Strange horrors tortured my soul, and it groaned and groaned, gaoled in that wolfish body. The wind whispered to me; with its myriad voices it spake to me and said, 'Go, search and kill.' And above these voices sounded the hideous laughter of an old man. I fled the moor—whither I knew not, nor knew I what motive lashed me on.

"I came to a river and I plunged in. A burning thirst consumed me, and I lapped the waters of the river—they were waves of flame, and they flashed around me and hissed, and what they said was, 'Go, search and kill,' and I heard the old man's laughter again.

A forest lay before me with its gloomy thickets and its sombre shadows—with its ravens, its vampires, its serpents, its reptiles, and all its hideous brood of night.

"A forest lay before me with its gloomy thickets and its sombre shadows—with its ravens, its vampires, its serpents, its reptiles, and all its hideous brood of night. I darted among its thorns and crouched amid the leaves, the nettles, and the brambles.

The owls hooted at me and the thorns pierced my flesh. 'Go, search and kill,' said everything. The hares sprang from my pathway; the other beasts ran bellowing away; every form of life shrieked in my ears—the curse was on me—I was the werewolf.

"On, on I went with the fleetness of the wind, and my soul groaned in its wolfish prison, and the winds and the waters and the trees bade me, 'Go, search and kill, thou accursed brute; go, search and kill.'

"Nowhere was there pity for the wolf; what mercy, thus, should I, the werewolf, show? The curse was on me and it filled me with a hunger and a thirst for blood. Skulking on my way within myself I cried, 'Let me have blood, oh, let me have human blood, that this wrath may be appeased, that this curse may be removed.'

"At last I came to the sacred grove. Sombre loomed the poplars, the oaks frowned upon me. Before me stood an old man—'twas he, grizzled and taunting, whose curse I bore. He feared me not. All other living things fled before me, but the old man feared me not. A maiden stood beside him. She did not see me, for she was blind.

"'Kill, kill,' cried the old man, and he pointed at the girl beside him.

"Hell raged within me—the curse impelled me—I sprang at her throat. I heard the old man's laughter once more, and then—then I awoke, trembling, cold, horrified."

Scarce was this dream told when Alfred strode that way.

"Now, by'r Lady," quoth he, "I bethink me never to have seen a sorrier twain."

Then Yseult told him of Harold's going away and how that Harold had besought her not to venture to the feast of Ste. Ælfreda in the sacred grove.

"These fears are childish," cried Alfred boastfully. "And thou sufferest me, sweet lady, I will bear thee company to the feast, and a score of my lusty yeomen with their good yew-bows and honest spears, they shall attend me. There be no werewolf, I trow, will chance about with us."

Whereat Yseult laughed merrily, and Harold said: "'T is well; thou shalt go to the sacred grove, and may my love and Heaven's grace forefend all evil."

Then Harold went to his abode, and he fetched old Siegfried's spear back unto Yseult, and he gave it into her two hands, saying, "Take this spear with thee to the feast to-morrow night. It is old Siegfried's spear, possessing mighty virtue and marvellous."

And Harold took Yseult to his heart and blessed her, and he kissed her upon her brow and upon her lips, saying, "Farewell, oh, my beloved. How wilt thou love me when thou know'st my sacrifice. Farewell, farewell forever, oh, alder-liefest mine."

So Harold went his way, and Yseult was lost in wonderment.

On the morrow night came Yseult to the sacred grove wherein the feast was spread, and she bore old Siegfried's spear with her in her girdle. Alfred attended her, and a score of lusty yeomen were with him. In the grove there was great merriment, and with singing and dancing and games withal did the honest folk celebrate the feast of the fair Ste. Ælfreda.

But suddenly a mighty tumult arose, and there were cries of "The werewolf!" "The werewolf!" Terror seized upon all—stout hearts were frozen with fear. Out from the further forest rushed the werewolf, wood wroth, bellowing hoarsely, gnashing his fangs and tossing hither and thither the yellow foam from his snapping jaws. He sought Yseult straight, as if an evil power drew him to the spot where she stood. But Yseult was not afeared; like a marble statue she stood and saw the werewolf's

And Yseult saw in the werewolf's eyes the eyes of some one she had seen and known, but 't was for an instant only, and then the eyes were no longer human, but wolfish in their ferocity.

coming. The yeomen, dropping their torches and casting aside their bows, had fled; Alfred alone abided there to do the monster battle.

At the approaching wolf he hurled his heavy lance, but as it struck the werewolf's bristling back the weapon was all to-shivered.

Then the werewolf, fixing his eyes upon Yseult, skulked for a moment in the shadow of the yews and thinking then of Harold's words, Yseult plucked old Siegfried's spear from her girdle, raised it on high, and with the strength of despair sent it hurtling through the air.

The werewolf saw the shining weapon, and a cry burst from his gaping throat—a cry of human agony. And Yseult saw in the werewolf's eyes the eyes of some one she had seen and known, but 't was for an instant only, and then the eyes were no longer human, but wolfish in their ferocity. A supernatural force seemed to speed the spear in its flight. With fearful precision the weapon smote home and buried itself by half its length in the werewolf's shaggy breast just above the heart, and then, with a monstrous sigh—as if he yielded up his life without regret—the werewolf fell dead in the shadow of the yews.

Then, ah, then in very truth there was great joy, and loud were the acclaims, while, beautiful in her trembling pallor, Yseult was led unto her home, where the people set about to give great feast to do her homage, for the werewolf was dead, and she it was that had slain him.

But Yseult cried out: "Go, search for Harold—go, bring him to me. Nor eat, nor sleep till he be found."

"Good my lady," quoth Alfred, "how can that be, since he hath betaken himself to Normandy?"

"I care not where he be," she cried. "My heart stands still until I look into his eyes again."

"Surely he hath not gone to Normandy," outspake Hubert. "This very eventide I saw him enter his abode."

They hastened thither—a vast company. His chamber door was barred.

"Harold, Harold, come forth!" they cried, as they beat upon the door, but no answer came to their calls and knockings. Afeared, they battered down the door, and when it fell they saw that Harold lay upon his bed.

"He sleeps," said one. "See, he holds a portrait in his hand—and it is her portrait. How fair he is and how tranquilly he sleeps."

But no, Harold was not asleep. His face was calm and beautiful, as if he dreamed of his beloved, but his raiment was red with the blood that streamed from a wound in his breast—a gaping, ghastly spear wound just above his heart.

A WOLF'S TALE

Most stories and films tend to depict werewolves as evil creatures, but in some, they can come across as largely sympathetic. One example would be Manly Banister's story, "Eena," that was published in 1947 and broke with tradition by following the story of a werewolf who is sympathetic and female. J.K. Rowling's werewolf character in the Harry Potter novels, Remus Lupin, is known to be entirely compassionate and understanding. In the hit show *Buffy the Vampire Slayer*, Oz is a werewolf who learns to control his wild impulses in order to win back Willow, the ex-girlfriend he adores.

9

HIRSUTE HISTORY

What would you not pay to see the moon rise if Nature had not improvidently made it a free entertainment!

—RICHARD LE GALLIENNE

Some of the scariest tales are those from the 16th and 17th centuries when, one can imagine, the hillsides ran rampant with wild beasts. It's only natural that werewolves were a feared predator and, whether natural or supernatural, they were certainly a very legitimate fear among villagers and royalty alike. The following are some of my favorite historical tales of terror!

Vampires, Witches, and Werewolves, Oh My!

Like witches and vampires, werewolves were often blamed for pestilence and wrong-doings round the village. Thievenne Paget was an infamous witch who also frequently transformed into a she-wolf. In her own confession, she states the devil often accompanied her on her raids slaying cattle, goats, and children. Her story is similar to that of Clauda Isan Prost who admitted to murdering five children in the same wolfish manner.

Get Behind Me, Satan

In the 17th century, French author Henri Bouget believed that Satan was responsible for entering the spirits of people while they were sleeping and transforming them into wolves. From there, he would do whatever evil deeds he had planned. According to Bouget, the devil could confuse the victims so much that they would wake up believing they really had been a wolf killing men and animals.

During the Middle Ages, most people believed Satan handcrafted werewolves and witches.

Tailor of Terror

On December 14, 1598, the Parliament of Paris sentenced a seemingly humble tailor to death by fire for practicing lycanthropy. His method involved luring children into his shop where he attacked them if they tried to escape. Typically, he'd tear them apart with his teeth to kill them, and then cut and cook the meat as if it'd come from cattle. Nobody knows the exact number of children he took, but authorities discovered a trunk full of bones in his cellar. By the end of the trial, the judges were so repulsed by the evidence that they had all the documents burned.

The Devil's Workhorse

During the winter of 1521, two Frenchmen, Peter the Great and Michel Verdung, were accused of witchcraft and cannibalism. Soon after the trial began, Peter confessed all of his crimes. He explained that nineteen years before, he was trying to find his lost sheep in a storm when three black horsemen approached him. They said they'd find the flock for him and give him some money. Four or five days later, as promised, Peter found his flock of sheep. Then he found out the three horsemen were servants of the devil. Because they treated him so well, Peter renounced Christianity and gave his soul to the devil.

After two years, he got tired of serving the devil and started going back to church. It was then he met Michel Verdung, who was sent to give Peter money and recruit him back to Satan's work. Soon after Michel's arrival, Peter began transforming into a wolf. Under Michel's guidance, he learned how to transform into a wolf and back into human form again. To transform, Michel could morph into a wolf with his clothes still on, while Peter had to be completely naked. Together, they'd go on raids. During one of his werewolf runs, Peter leaped on a young boy, intending to eat him, but the boy let out such a loud cry, he retreated immediately. Another time, he and Michel tore a woman to pieces while she was working in her garden. They strangled and devoured a young girl, only leaving her arm as evidence.

A Declaration of Declawing

In the early autumn of 1573, French peasants were ordered by Parliament to hunt down werewolves that were running wild across the country. They'd been known to kidnap children and eat them, so the peasants were authorized to do whatever was necessary in order to capture the werewolves.

Hermit the Fog

In a small hovel far from any roads in rural France, there lived a secluded old man. The man, Gilles Garnier, usually appeared ill and walked with a protruding stoop in his back. Because he had long grey hair, a sickly appearance, and an introverted personality, he was named the Hermit of St. Bonnot by local townspeople. They hardly ever heard from him, so no one would expect any wrongdoing on his part. But one day, some peasants were walking down the road by the hermit's house when they heard a child screaming and the deep howls of a wolf. They ran to the scene and found the little girl trying to defend herself against the monstrous creature, although she'd already sustained severe injuries. When the werewolf saw the peasants approaching, he fled on all fours. However, it was dark and foggy out so they could not clearly identify him.

About a week later, a ten-year-old boy went missing and was last seen not far from the hermit's hovel. The Hermit of St. Bonnot was then seized and brought to trial. It was reported in court that a young girl was walking about a mile from the hermit's house when a wolf savagely ate her. Eight days later, another girl was kidnapped but managed to escape when three witnesses appeared just as she was about to be

eaten. Soon after that, a ten-year-old boy was found dead with the majority of his midsection devoured. After all the evidence was compiled, the hermit fully believed he committed each act in the form of a wolf and confessed to every murder.

It Runs in the Family

In 1598, a poor girl named Pernette Gandillon ran around the country on all fours, believing she was a wolf. One day she was running through the fields when she spied two children plucking wild strawberries. Blinded by a thirst for blood, she pounced on the little girl but was gashed in the side by the girl's little brother, who was carrying a knife. Pernette wrestled the knife from the boy and stabbed him in the neck, killing him instantly. When the townspeople caught wind of this, they hunted Pernette down and tore her to pieces.

Shortly after the horrifying incident, Pernette's older brother, Pierre, was accused of witchcraft. He was charged for leading children to the Sabbath and encouraging them to run around the country as if they were wolves. Pierre used a salve to coat the children's bodies and transform them into werewolves. He was able to transform as well and admitted to devouring both animals and humans. Pierre also used the salve to anoint his son, Georges, who admitted going to Sabbath in the form of a wolf. He also admitted to killing two goats during one of his escapades.

In prison, Pierre and Georges behaved like maniacs and would not stop crawling around their cells on all fours and howling loudly. Covering their faces, arms, and legs were scars that they'd gotten from dogs attacking them during their raids. When the trial was finally over, Pierre and Georges were hung and burned.

SEXY SHAG

In the same way vampires have been linked to sexuality, so have werewolves. Your typical werewolf is hyper-masculine, as opposed to the suave, sensual nature of a vampire, and can be extremely muscular and violent. According to some stories, a man can become a werewolf if he is too rough, sexually deviant, or simply goes against community standards.

TROUBLED TEENS

In the Channel Islands off the coast of France, 16th-century teenagers known to break curfews and roam around town at night were commonly called werewolves. (By this definition, yours truly would have been considered a werewolf!) A similar belief was that criminals could turn into werewolves due to their bad behavior.

> There are historical documents claiming at least two different saints transformed sinners into wolves as a form of punishment.

10

THE WEREWOLF
OF THE NORTH

Give them great meals of beef and iron and steel,
they will eat like wolves and fight like devils.

—William Shakespeare, from *Henry V*

Should you ever find yourself on a lovely country lane, ambling along and enjoying the late afternoon autumnal air, only to quietly realize that you have gone far, far from the path you'd originally taken (the path that leads to the expansive estate you've been guesting at, recuperating from your nervous breakdown), you would be well-advised to head quickly back in what you assume is the proper direction. Soon the sun will fall behind the darkening tree line, and you will be on the edge of a dreary wood, where all manner of creatures dwell. Their eyes will flash as you stumble along, desperate to find the way that seems familiar. Most of these creatures are harmless. There are raccoons, those nocturnal scoundrels, leathery winged bats (you aren't afraid of bats, are you?), and hooting owls to mark the evening's arrival. All of these creatures are spooky, perhaps, but not dangerous. But then there are also creatures in that wood that you do not wish to encounter. Vicious beasts of unimaginable size, with sharp claws and long fangs, hungry and ready to kill. Among them you may find the werewolf.

Sabine Baring-Gould was an eclectic man. Born in England in 1834, he is best known for the hymns he composed, among them the infamous "Onward, Christian Soldiers." He was married for nearly fifty years and fathered fifteen children. He was a collector of stories and folk songs as well as an accomplished novelist, and was known to write while standing. This selection of folklore of the Scandinavian werewolves is part of his greater work, *The Book of Werewolves*, which was published in 1865 and is still one of the largest studies of werewolf lore to this day. He died in 1924 and was buried next to his wife.

Was he afraid of that wild beast that was just at the edge of the tundra? Did he believe? If you read on, I think you'll agree that werewolves—whether dangerous or desirous—are indeed quite real.

THE ORIGIN OF THE SCANDINAVIAN WERE-WOLF

by Sabine Baring-Gould

In Norway and Iceland certain men were said to be *eigi einhamir*, not of one skin, an idea which had its roots in paganism. The full form of this strange superstition was, that men could take upon them other bodies, and the natures of those beings whose bodies they assumed. The second adopted shape was called by the same name as the original shape, *hamr*, and the expression made use of to designate the transition from one body to another, was at *skipta hömum*, or *at hamaz*; whilst the expedition made in the second form, was the *hamför*. By this transfiguration extraordinary powers were acquired; the natural strength of the individual was doubled, or quadrupled; he acquired the strength of the beast in whose body he travelled, in addition to his own, and a man thus invigorated was called *hamrammr*.

The manner in which the change was effected, varied. At times, a dress of skin was cast over the body, and at once the transformation was complete; at others, the human body was deserted, and the soul entered the second form, leaving the first body in a cataleptic state, to all appearance dead. The second hamr was either borrowed or created for the purpose. There was yet a third manner of producing this effect—it was by incantation; but then the form of the individual remained unaltered, though the eyes of all beholders were charmed so that they could only perceive him under the selected form.

Having assumed some bestial shape, the man who is *eigi einhammr* is only to be recognized by his eyes, which by no power can be changed. He then pursues his course, follows the instincts of the beast whose body he has taken, yet without quenching his own intelligence. He is able to do what the body of the animal can do, and do what he, as man, can do as well. He may fly or swim, if he is in the shape of bird or fish; if he has taken the form of a wolf, or if he goes on a *gandreið*, or wolf's-ride, he is full of the rage and malignity of the creatures whose powers and passions he has assumed.

At times, a dress of skin was cast over the body, and at once the transformation was complete; at others, the human body was deserted, and the soul entered the second form, leaving the first body in a cataleptic state, to all appearance dead.

The introduction of Sœmund tells us that these charming young ladies were caught when they had laid their swanskins beside them on the shore, and were consequently not in a condition to fly.

In like manner were wolves' dresses used. The following curious passage is from the wild Saga of the Völsungs:

"It is now to be told that Sigmund thought Sinfjötli too young to help him in his revenge, and he wished first to test his powers; so during the summer they plunged deep into the wood and slew men for their goods, and Sigmund saw that he was quite of the Völsung stock. . . . Now it fell out that as they went through the forest, collecting monies, that they lighted on a house in which were two men sleeping, with great gold rings on them; they had dealings with witchcraft, for wolf-skins hung up in the house above them; it was the tenth day on which they might come out of their second state. They were kings' sons. Sigmund and Sinfjötli got into the habits, and could not get out of them again, and the nature of the original beasts came over them, and they howled as wolves— they learned both of them to howl. Now they went into the forest, and each took his own course; they made the agree-  ment together that they should try their strength against as many as seven men, but not more, and that he who was ware of strife should utter his wolf's howl.

"'Do not fail in this,' said Sigmund, 'for you are young and daring, and men would be glad to chase you.' Now each went his own course; and after that they had parted Sigmund found men, so he howled; and when Sinfjötli heard that, he ran up and slew them all—then they separated. And Sinfjötli had not been long in the wood before he met with eleven men; he fell upon them and slew them every one. Then he was tired, so he flung himself under an oak to rest. Up came Sigmund and said, 'Why did you not call out?' Sinfjötli replied, 'What was the need of asking your help to kill eleven men?'

"Sigmund flew at him and rent him so that he fell, for he had bitten through his throat. That day they could not leave their wolf-forms. Sigmund laid him on his back and bare him home to the hall, and sat beside him, and said, 'Deuce take the wolf-forms!'" —Völsung Saga ...

Sigmund and Sinfjötli got into the habits, and could not get out of them again, and the nature of the original beasts came over them, and they howled as wolves—they learned both of them to howl.

There is another story bearing on the subject in the Hrolfs Saga Kraka, which is pretty; it is as follows:

"In the north of Norway, in upland-dales, reigned a king called Hring; and he had a son named Björn. Now it fell out that the queen died, much lamented by the king, and by all. The people advised him to marry again, and so he sent men south to get him a wife. A gale and fierce storm fell upon them, so that they had to turn the helm, and run before the wind, and so they came north to Finnmark, where they spent the winter. One day they went inland, and came to a house in which sat two beautiful women, who greeted them well, and inquired whence they had come. They replied by giving an account of their journey and their errand, and then asked the women who they were, and why they were alone, and far from the haunts of men, although they were so comely and engaging. The elder replied—that her name was Ingibjorg, and that her daughter was called Hvit, and that she was the Finn king's sweetheart. The messengers decided that they would return home, if Hvit would come with them and marry King Hring. She agreed, and they took her with them and met the king who was pleased with her, and had his wedding feast made, and said that he cared not though she was not rich. But the king was very old, and that the queen soon found out.

"There was a Carle who had a farm not far from the king's dwelling; he had a wife, and a daughter, who was but a child, and her name was Bera; she was very young and lovely. Björn the king's son, and Bera the Carle's daughter, were wont, as children, to play together, and they loved each other well. The Carle was well to do, he had been out harrying in his young days, and he was a doughty champion. Björn and Bera loved each other more and more, and they were often together.

"Time passed, and nothing worth relating occurred; but Björn, the king's son, waxed strong and tall; and he was well skilled in all manly exercises.

"King Hring was often absent for long, harrying foreign shores, and Hvit remained at home and governed the land. She was not liked of the people. She was always very pleasant with Björn, but he cared little for her. It fell out once that the King Hring went abroad, and he spake with his queen that Björn should remain at home with her, to assist in the government, for he thought it advisable, the queen being haughty and inflated with pride.

"The king told his son Björn that he was to remain at home, and rule the land with the queen; Björn replied that he disliked the plan, and that he had no love for the queen; but the king was inflexible, and left the land with a great following. Björn walked home after his conversation with the king, and went up to his place, ill-pleased and red as blood. The queen came to speak with him, and to cheer him; and spake friendly with him, but he bade her be off. She obeyed him that time. She often came to talk with him, and said how much pleasanter it was for them to be together, than to have an old fellow like Hring in the house.

"Björn resented this speech, and struck her a box in the ear, and bade her depart, and he spurned her from him. She replied that this was ill-done to drive and thrust her away: and 'You think it better, Björn, to sweetheart a Carle's daughter, than to have my love and favour, a fine piece of condescension and a disgrace it is to you! But, before long, something will stand in the way of your fancy, and your folly.' Then she struck at him with a wolf-skin glove, and said, that he should become a rabid and grim wild bear; and 'You shall eat nothing but your father's sheep, which you shall slay for your food, and never shall you leave this state.'

"After that, Björn disappeared, and none knew what had become of him; and men sought but found him not, as was to be expected. We must now relate how that the king's sheep were slaughtered, half a score at a time, and it was all the work of a grey bear, both huge and grimly.

"One evening it chanced that the Carle's daughter saw this savage bear coming towards her, looking tenderly at her, and she fancied that she recognized the eyes of Björn, the king's son, so she made a slight attempt to escape; then the beast retreated, but she followed it, till she came to a cave. Now when she entered the cave there stood before her a man, who greeted Bera, the Carle's daughter; and she recognized him, for he was Björn, Hring's son. Overjoyed were they to meet. So they were together in the cave awhile, for she would not part from him when she had the chance of being with him; but he said that this was not proper that she should be there by him, for by day he was a beast, and by night a man.

Then she struck at him with a wolf-skin glove, and said, that he should become a rabid and grim wild bear; and 'You shall eat nothing but your father's sheep, which you shall slay for your food, and never shall you leave this state.'

"Hring returned from his harrying, and he was told the news, of what had taken place during his absence; how that Björn, his son, had vanished, and also, how that a monstrous beast was up the country, and was destroying his flocks. The queen urged the king to have the beast slain, but he delayed awhile.

"One night, as Bera and Björn were together, he said to her: 'Methinks to-morrow will be the day of my death, for they will come out to hunt me down. But for myself I care not, for it is little pleasure to live with this charm upon me, and my only comfort is that we are together; but now our union must be broken. I will give you the ring which is under my left hand. You will see the troop of hunters to-morrow coming to seek me; and when I am dead go to the king, and ask him to give you what is under the beast's left front leg. He will consent.'

"He spoke to her of many other things, till the bear's form stole over him, and he went forth a bear. She followed him, and saw that a great body of hunters had come over the mountain ridges, and had a number of dogs with them. The bear rushed away from the cavern, but the dogs and the king's men came upon him, and there was a desperate struggle. He wearied many men before he was brought to bay, and had slain all the dogs. But now they made a ring about him, and he ranged around it, but could see no means of escape, so he turned to where the king stood, and he seized

a man who stood next him, and rent him asunder; then was the bear so exhausted that he cast himself down flat, and, at once, the men rushed in upon him and slew him. The Carle's daughter saw this, and she went up to the king, and said, 'Sire! wilt thou grant me that which is under the bear's left fore-shoulder?' The king consented. By this time his men had nearly flayed the bear; Bera went up and plucked away the ring, and kept it, but none saw what she took, nor had they looked for anything. The king asked her who she was, and she gave a name, but not her true name.

"The king now went home, and Bera was in his company. The queen was very joyous, and treated her well, and asked who she was; but Bera answered as before.

"The queen now made a great feast, and had the bear's flesh cooked for the banquet. The Carle's daughter was in the bower of the queen, and could not escape, for the queen had a suspicion who she was. Then she came to Bera with a dish, quite unexpectedly, and on it was bear's flesh, and she bade Bera eat it. She would not do so. 'Here is a marvel!' said the queen; 'you reject the offer which a queen herself deigns to make to you. Take it at once, or something worse will befall you.' She bit before her, and she ate of that bite; the queen cut another piece, and looked into her mouth; she saw that one little grain of the bite had gone down, but Bera spat out all the rest from her mouth, and said she would take no more, though she were tortured or killed.

"'Maybe you have had sufficient,' said the queen, and she laughed." —(Hrolfs Saga Kraka, condensed)

GHOST WOLF

Some refer to the Stull Cemetery in Kansas City, Kansas, perhaps one of the most fantastical of all haunted cemeteries, as the Gates of Hell, the Cemetery of the Damned, and the Seventh Gate to Hell. The devil himself is said to roam amongst the tombs. The devil's child is also said to dwell here, along with a boy who can change himself into a werewolf, and the ghost of a witch.

Brrrr

Cold yet? You'll be wishing you had a nice coat of fur yourself by the time you get through the following passage by Irish author Elliott O'Donnell, whom we first met in Part One: Banshees. O'Donnell was a folklorist and paranormal investigator who also, seemingly, believed in werewolves. Of particular note is his claim that "in Iceland there are both lycanthropous streams and flowers, and that they differ little if at all from those to be met with in other countries." In fact, he is referring to numerous accounts that there are plants and waters (streams tainted by plants' roots perhaps) that can cause an otherwise ordinary human to turn into a werewolf. I wonder if, as is so often the case in Nature, there are anti-dotes in these mysterious waters and flora as well.

Of note in the following passage is O'Donnell's reference to the bersekir of Iceland. Bersekir were Norse warriors that traditionally worked themselves into states of extreme rage before battle, and it is believed that many actually ingested herbs or drank water laced with a sort of trance-inducing drug. Could they have been ingesting the same lycanthro-pous flowers or waters that O'Donnell says turn one into a furious werewolf? And more importantly, do those flowers still grow, buried deep beneath the winter's snow, waiting for next year's victim of lycanthropy?

Werwolves in Iceland, Lapland, and Finland
by Elliott O'Donnell

The Bersekir of Iceland are credited with the rare property of dual metamorphosis—that is to say, they are credited with the power of being able to adopt the individual forms of two animals—the bear and the wolf.

For substantiation as to the *bona-fide* existence of this rare property of dual metamorphosis one has only to refer to the historical literature of the country (the authenticity of which is beyond dispute), wherein many cases of it are recorded.

The following story, illustrative of dual metamorphosis, was told to me on fairly good authority.

A very unprepossessing Bersekir, named Rerir, falling in love with Signi, the beautiful daughter of a neighbouring Bersekir, proposed to her and was scornfully rejected. Smarting under the many insults that had been heaped on him—for Signi had a most cutting tongue—Rerir, who, like most of the Bersekir, was both a werwolf and a wer-bear, resolved to be revenged. Assuming the shape of a bear—the animal he deemed the more formidable—Rerir stole to the house where Signi and her parents lived, and climbing on the roof, tore away at it with his claws till he had made a hole big enough to admit him. Dropping through the aperture he had thus effected, he alighted on the top of some one in bed—one of the servants of the house—whom he hugged to death before she had time to utter a cry. He then stole out into the passage and made his way, cautiously and noiselessly, to the room in which he imagined Signi slept. Here, however, instead of finding the object of his passions, he came upon her parents, one of whom—the mother—was awake; and aiming a blow at the latter's head, he crushed in her skull

with one stroke of his powerful paw. The noise awoke Signi's father, who, taking in the situation at a glance, also metamorphosed into a bear and straightway closed with his assailant. A desperate encounter between the two wer-animals now commenced, and the whole household, aroused from their slumber, came trooping in. For some time the issue of the combat was dubious, both adversaries being fairly well matched. But at length Rerir began to prevail, and Signi's father cried out for some one to help him. Then Signi, anxious to save her parent's life, seized a knife, and, aiming a frantic blow, inadvertently struck her father, who instantly sank on the ground, leaving her at the mercy of his furious opponent.

A desperate encounter between the two wer-animals now commenced, and the whole household, aroused from their slumber, came trooping in.

With a loud snarl of triumph, Rerir rushed at the girl, and was bearing her triumphantly away, when the cook—an old woman who had followed the fortunes of the Bersekir all her life—had a sudden inspiration. Standing on a shelf in the corner of the room was a jar containing a preparation of sulphur, asafœtida, and castoreum, which her mistress had always given her to understand was a preventive against evil spirits. Snatching it up, she darted after the wer-bear and flung the contents of it in its face, just as it was about to descend the stairs with Signi. In a moment there was a sudden and startling metamorphosis, and in the place of the bear stood the ugly, misshapen man, Rerir.

The hunchback now would gladly have departed without attempting further mischief; for although the household boasted no man apart from its incapacitated master, there were still three formidable women and some big dogs to be faced.

But to let him escape, after the irreparable harm he had done, was the very last thing Signi would permit; and with an air of stern authority she commanded the servants to fall on him with any weapons they could find, whilst she would summon the hounds.

Now, indeed, the tables were completely turned. Rerir was easily overpowered and bound securely hand and foot by Signi and her servants, and after undergoing a brief trial the following morning he was summarily executed.

Those Icelanders who possessed the property of metamorphosis into wolves and bears (they were always of the male sex), more often than not used it for the purpose of either wreaking vengeance or of executing justice. The terrible temper—for the rage of the Bersekir has been a byword for centuries—commonly attributed to Icelanders and Scandinavians in general, is undoubtedly traceable to the werwolves and wer-bears into which the Bersekirs metamorphosed.

It is said that in Iceland there are both lycanthropous streams and flowers, and that they differ little if at all from those to be met with in other countries.

HOWLING GOOD TIME

The werewolf is nearly inseparable from its howl. According to Fred H. Harrington, Professor of Ethology at Mt. Saint Vincent University in Nova Scotia, howling is what keeps a wolf and his pack together. Some scholars have suggested that howling promotes social bonds between wolves and the pack that howls the loudest usually stays together the longest. Howling is undoubtedly a good method for communication in a wolf pack. Werewolves have to cover huge areas of land in order to find food, so it isn't uncommon for them to separate. While werewolves have a variety of calls for different communication purposes, howling is by far the best way to communicate over long distances.

Wolves have to be careful about where and when they howl, though, because other wolves in the areas can hear it and get mixed signals. A wolf separated from his pack might revisit an old meeting site and howl for hours, but this can strike fear in wolves from a competing pack, causing them to flee or attack. Pups in particular will respond to howls whether they're coming from within their pack or not because they haven't learned to distinguish the subtle differences between howls yet. This can be dangerous because young pups might give away a pack's location when they are trying to be stealthy.

The Werwolves of Lapland

In Lapland werwolves are still much to the fore. In many families the property is hereditary, whilst it is not infrequently sought and acquired through the practice of Black Magic. Though, perhaps, more common among males, there are, nevertheless, many instances of it among females.

The following case comes from the country bordering on Lake Enara.

The child of a peasant woman named Martha, just able to trot alone, and consequently left to wander just where it pleased, came home one morning with its forehead apparently licked raw, all its fingers more or less injured, and two of them seemingly sucked and mumbled to a mere pulp.

On being interrogated as to what had happened, it told a most astounding tale: A very beautiful lady had picked it up and carried it away to her house, where she had put it in a room with her three children, who were all very pretty and daintily dressed. At sunset, however, both the lady and her children metamorphosed into wolves, and would undoubtedly have eaten it, had they not satiated their appetites on a portion of a girl which had been kept over from the preceding day. The newcomer was intended for their meal on the morrow, and obeying the injunctions of their mother, the young werwolves had forborne to devour the child, though they had all tasted it.

The child's parents were simply dumbfounded—they could scarcely credit their senses—and made their offspring repeat its narrative over and over again. And as it stuck to what it had said, they ultimately concluded that it was true, and that the lady described could be none other than Madame Tonno, the wife of their landlord and patron—a person of immense importance in the neighbourhood.

But what could they do? How could they protect their children from another raid?

To accuse the lady, who was rich and influential, of being a werwolf would be useless. No one would believe them—no one dare believe them—and they would be severely punished for their indiscretion. Being poor, they were entirely at her mercy, and if she chose to eat their children, they could not prevent her, unless they could catch her in the act.

One evening the mother was washing clothes before the door of her house, with her second child, a little girl of four years of age, playing about close by. The cottage stood in a lonely part of the estate, forming almost an island in the midst of low boggy ground; and there was no house nearer than that of M. Tonno. Martha, bending over her wash-tub, was making every effort to complete her task, when a fearful cry made her look up, and there was the child, gripped by one shoulder, in the jaws of a great she-wolf, the arm that was free extended towards her. Martha was so close that she managed to clutch a bit of the child's clothing in one hand, whilst with the other she beat the brute with all her might to

A fearful cry made her look up, and there was the child, gripped by one shoulder, in the jaws of a great she-wolf.

make it let go its hold. But all in vain: the relentless jaws did not show the slightest sign of relaxing, and with a saturnine glitter in its deep-set eyes it emitted a hoarse burr-burr, and set off at full speed towards the forest, dragging the mother, who was still clinging to the garment of her child, with it.

But they did not long continue thus. The wolf turned into some low-lying uneven track, and Martha, falling over the jagged trunk of a tree, found herself lying on the ground with only a little piece of torn clothing tightly clasped in her hand. Hitherto, comforted by Martha's presence, the little one had not uttered a sound; but now, feeling itself deserted, it gave vent to the most heartrending screams—screams that abruptly disturbed the silence of that lonely spot and pierced to the depths of Martha's soul. In an instant she rose, and, dashing on, bounded over stock and stone, tearing herself pitiably, but heeding it not in her intense anxiety to save her child. But the wolf had now increased its speed; the undergrowth was thick, the ground heavier, and soon screams became her only guide. Still on and on she dashed, now snatching up a little shoe which was clinging to the bushes, now shrieking with agony as she saw fragments of the child's hair and clothes on the low jagged boughs obstructing her path. On, on, on, until the screams grew fainter, then louder, and then ceased altogether.

Late that night the husband, Max, found his wife lying dead, just outside the grounds of his patron's château.

Guessing what had happened, and having but one thought in his mind—namely, revenge—Max, arming himself with the branch of a tree, marched boldly up to the house, and rapped loudly at the door.

M. Tonno answered this peremptory summons himself, and demanded in an angry voice what Max meant by daring to announce himself thus.

Max pointed in the direction of the corpse. "That!" he shrieked; "that is the reason of my visit. Madame Tonno is a werwolf—she has murdered both my wife and child, and I am here to demand justice."

"Come inside," M. Tonno said, the tone of his voice suddenly changing. "We can discuss the matter indoors in the privacy of my study." And he conducted Max to a room in the rear of the house.

But no sooner had Max crossed the threshold than the door was slammed on him, and he found himself a prisoner. He turned to the window, but there was no hope there—it was heavily barred. But although a peasant—and a fool, so he told himself, to have thus deliberately walked into a trap—Max was not altogether without wits, and he searched the room thoroughly, eventually discovering a loose board. Tearing it up, he saw that the space under the floor—that is to say, between the floor and the foundation of the house—was just deep enough for him to lie there at full length. Here, then, was a possible avenue of escape. Setting to work, he succeeded, after much effort, in wrenching up another board, and then another, and getting into the excavation thus made, he worked his way along on his stomach, until he came to a grating, which, to his utmost joy, proved to be loose. It was but the work of a few minutes to force it out and to dislodge a few bricks, and Max was once again free. His one idea now was to tell his tale to his brother peasants and rouse them to immediate action, and with this end in view he set off running at full speed to the nearest settlement.

The peasants of Lapland are slow and stolid and take a lot of rousing, but when once they are roused, few people are so terrible.

Fortunately for Max, he was not the only sufferer; several other people in the neighbourhood had lately lost their children, and the story he told found ready credence. In less than an hour a large body of men and women, armed with every variety of weapon, from a sword to a pitchfork, had gathered together, and setting off direct to the château, they surrounded it on all sides, and forcing an entrance, seized M. Tonno and his werwolf wife and werwolf children, and binding them hand and foot, led them to the shores of Lake

Enara and drowned them. They then went back to the house and, setting fire to it, burned it to the ground, thus making certain of destroying any werwolf influence it might still contain.

With this wholesale extermination a case that may be taken as a characteristic type of Lapland lycanthropy in all its grim and sordid details concludes.

Finland Werwolves

Finland teems with stories of werwolves—stories ancient and modern, for the werwolf is said to still flourish in various parts of the country.

The property is not restricted to one sex; it is equally common to both. Spells and various forms of exorcism are used, and certain streams are held to be lycanthropous.

However, in Finland as in Scandinavia, it is very difficult to procure information as to werwolves. The common peasant, who alone knows anything about the anomaly, is withheld by superstition from even mentioning its name; and if he mentions a werwolf at all, designates him only as the "old one," or the "grey one," or the "great dog," feeling that to call this terror by its true name is a sure way to exasperate it. It is only by strategy one learns from a peasant that when a fine young ox is found in the morning breathing hard, his hide bathed in foam, and with every sign of fright and exhaustion, while, perhaps, only one trifling wound is discovered on the whole body, which swells and inflames as if poison had been infused, the animal generally dying before night; and that when, on examination of the corpse, the intestines are found to be torn as with the claws of a wolf, and the whole body is in a state of inflammation, it is accounted certain that the mischief has been caused by a werwolf.

It is thus a werwolf serves his quarry when he kills for the mere love of killing, and not for food.

In Finland, perhaps more than in other countries, werwolves are credited with demoniacal power, and old women who possess the property of metamorphosing into wolves are said to be able to paralyse cattle and children with their eyes, and to have poison in their nails, one wound from which causes certain death.

To illustrate the foregoing I have selected an incident which happened near Diolen, a village on the eastern shore of the Gulf of Finland, at the distance of about a hundred wersts from the ancient city of Mawa. Here vegetation is of a more varied and luxuriant kind than is usually found in the Northern latitude; the oak and the bela, intermingled with rich plots of grass, grow at the very edge of the sea—a phenomenon accountable for by the fact that the Baltic is tideless.

For about half a werst in breadth, the shore continues a level, luxuriant stretch, when it suddenly rises in three successive cliffs, each about a hundred feet in height, and placed about the same space of half a werst, one behind the other, like huge steps leading to the table-land above. In some places the rocks are completely hidden from the view by a thick fence of trees, which take root at their base, while each level is covered by a minute forest of firs, in which grow a variety of herbs and shrubs, including the English whitethorn, and wild strawberries.

It was to gather the latter that Savanich and his seven-year-old son, Peter, came one afternoon early in summer. They had filled two baskets and were contemplating returning home with their spoil, when Caspan, the big sheepdog, uttered a low growl.

"Hey, Caspan, what is it?" Peter cried. "Footsteps! And such curious ones!"

"They are curious," Savanich said, bending down to examine them. "They are larger and coarser than those of Caspan, longer in shape, and with a deep indentation of the ball of the foot. They are those of a wolf—an old one, because of the deepness of the tracks. Old wolves walk heavy. And here's a wound the brute has got in its paw. See! there is a slight irregularity on the print of the hind feet, as if from a dislocated claw. We must be on our guard.

A couple of thrusts from his knife stretched the wolf on the ground, when, to his utmost horror, it suddenly metamorphosed into a hideous old hag.

Wolves are hungry now: the waters have driven them up together, and the cattle are not let out yet. The beast is not far off, either. An old wolf like this will prowl about for days together, round the same place, till he picks up something."

"I hope it won't attack us, father," Peter said, catching hold of Savanich by the hand. "What should you do if it did?"

But before Savanich could reply, Caspan gave a loud bark and dashed into the thicket, and the next moment a terrible pandemonium of yells, and snorts, and sharp howls filled the air. Drawing his knife from its sheath, and telling Peter to keep close at his heels, Savanich followed Caspan and speedily came upon the scene of the encounter. Caspan had hold of a huge grey wolf by the neck, and was hanging on to it like grim death, in spite of the brute's frantic efforts to free itself.

There was but little doubt that the brave dog would have, eventually, paid the penalty for its rashness—for the wolf had mauled it badly, and it was beginning to show signs of exhaustion through loss of blood—had not Savanich arrived in the nick of time. A couple of thrusts from his knife stretched the wolf on the ground, when, to his utmost horror, it suddenly metamorphosed into a hideous old hag.

"A werwolf!" Savanich gasped, crossing himself. "Get out of her way, Peter, quick!"

But it was too late. Thrusting out a skinny hand, the hag scratched Peter on the ankle with the long curved, poisonous nail of her forefinger. Then, with an evil smile on her lips, she turned over on her back, and expired. And before Peter could be got home he, too, was dead.

11

NATURAL CAUSES OF
LYCANTHROPY

I have actually gotten to like fear.

—Pearl White

We are all werewolves. At least, according to Sabine Baring-Gould, all humans have the capacity for licentious lust and blood thirst. We just possess it in varying degrees. From the wicked blood baths of Madame Bathory, to the stabbing knife of Jack the Ripper, to the young child whose curiosity drives him to pluck the wings from a fly, there are various gradients of these destructive urges. So by this measure, having werewolf-like urges is a very realistic thing.

Werewolves are both victims and predators. The abuses of an early childhood can lead to the path of the werewolf. The madness of an iron-deficient pregnancy can bring a woman to bear her teeth in a beast-like fashion. Here are a few stories about the natural, and somewhat disturbing, causes of werewolfism.

CLERGY URGE

Robert Burton, a clergyman and scholar, believed lycanthropy to be a type of disease that brought on madness. In his 1621 book, *Anatomy of Melancholy*, he blames the disease on a variety of things from sorcerers and witches to poor diet, pollution, insomnia, and lack of exercise. In the 19th century, French occultist Eliphas Levi wrote *Mysteries of Magic*, a book hypothesizing that some men have savage instincts that lead them to believe they are actually wolves. He believed the human body was capable of injuring itself (resulting in apparent wolf bites) under extreme anxiety. Many other doctors during this time suggested lycanthropes treat themselves with baths, purging, bleeding, dietary supplements, and applying opium to the nostrils.

THOUGHT MONSTERS

The connection between werewolves and rough behavior has clear ties to modern psychology. It has metaphorical value in the sense that you can see werewolf tendencies reflecting the human struggle to come to terms with our animal nature. As a man transforms into a werewolf, his most primal instincts take over, which obviously parallels puberty. Similar to the process of puberty, the body endures dramatic changes that are beyond one's control. In some cases, the changes a werewolf goes through are used as a metaphor for menstruation. According to a monthly cycle, a woman's body changes in ways that are central to her womanhood in the same way a werewolf undergoes cyclical changes that are central to his or her identity.

Despite their status as monsters, most people can identify with werewolves. Whether you have a tough time controlling your emotional outbursts, or you have trouble reeling in your animalistic nature, chances are you can empathize with at least one werewolf trait.

ABBY NORMAL: OTHER REAL DISEASES THAT PERPETUATE BELIEF IN WEREWOLVES

There is the well-known disease, hypertrichosis, "Wolfitis," which refers to excessive body hair. Usually, the term is

used to refer to an abnormal amount of body hair that is unwanted, affecting a generalized area like the entire torso and limbs, or localized, affecting a specific area of the body. Severe hypertrichosis involves excessive animalistic hair covering the entire face and body.

In very rare cases, there is such a thing called the Human Werewolf Syndrome, in which werewolves can transform from human to wolf form and still maintain human consciousness. It is believed this condition can only occur when a werewolf child is born to werewolf parents.

Other Real Things that Perpetuate Belief in Werewolves

Ergot poisoning: Ergot is the result of a fungus that grows on grains like barley and wheat. Eating it mistakenly can cause hallucinations, and LSD was initially made from ergot compounds. This is thought to be the cause behind some witch trials.

Rabies: Rabies is typically transmitted through biting. Rabies kills unless treated immediately and can cause agitation and hallucinations. For those bitten by rabid dogs, they might display werewolf tendencies.

Wolf hybrids: Aggressive hybrids of wolves and dogs have been known to attack villages without being provoked.

No Duh, Duke

A professor from Duke University claimed that changes in the brain's electrical activity coincide with lunar phases. According to other similar studies, certain lunar cycles have been connected to increases in strokes and seizures. During a full moon, drugs have been known to have greater effect, hormones become more active, and the body's metabolism experiences a slight increase. Police records show that the most violent crimes tend to happen during full moon phases. In New York City, studies have shown that instances of arson double during a full moon, and the nationwide murder rate jumps by 50 percent during this time as well.

Traits

In European folklore, werewolves were believed to have wolfish traits, even when in their human form. Some of these traits included having a unibrow, long curved fingernails,

large ears, and a loping stride. One method used to reveal a werewolf involved peeling back a person's skin to see if there was fur on the underside. One Russian superstition speaks of a werewolf being revealed by bristles under the tongue.

A werewolf's appearance is thought to be not much different from that of a regular wolf, with the exception that a werewolf does not have a long, bushy tail. Additionally, werewolves tend to be tall and retain human eyes and vocal chords. In some Swedish legends, a werewolf was distinguished from other wolves by the irregular way it ran on three legs and stretched one leg back in an effort to look like a tail.

Upon returning to human form, werewolves have been known to become weak and fatigued, sometimes undergoing extreme anxiety and depression. In European folklore, werewolves had the revolting habit of feasting on recently interred bodies. This trait in particular was thoroughly documented in the 19th-century book *Annales Medicopsychologiques*.

BE THE CHANGE: SHAPESHIFTERS

Navajo mythology suggests you can magically transform into any animal of your choosing by wearing that animal's skin. These people were known as "skinwalkers" and were not surprisingly considered evil. Becoming a skinwalker took considerable skill and sacrifice, while real werewolfism was considered a curse that allowed for little to no control.

You can find werewolf legends in almost every culture, many dating back to ancient times. One of those legends takes place in what is now Wisconsin. According to the story, elite members of an early Native American tribe had the ability to transform into wolves under the guidance of the spirit Wisakachek. A shape-shifter who sought refuge in the woods, Wisakachek had friendly relationships with humans, although his default physical form was that of a wolf. One day when he took the form of a man, he came across two tribe members hunting in the woods. The boys, Keme and Matchitehew (a Native American name meaning "boy with an evil heart"), just caught a deer when Wisakachek approached them. He announced himself as a lonely, hungry wanderer, so the boys, thinking he was a stranger, offered him some of the deer meat.

Weeks later, Wisakachek came across the same boys again. Matchitehew saw him and explained that, since they last met, they were unable to catch another deer and were near starvation. Remembering how generous the boys had been before, Wisakachek decided to share his transformative powers. In front of their amazed eyes, he transformed into a wolf and back into a human again before they gratefully agreed to learn his ways. The only condition Wisakachek gave the boys was that they could only use their wolf personas to hunt for food, not to harm any human beings.

Months went by and the boys were able to feed their entire tribe with their new powers. Everything seemed to be going well until, one day, Matchitehew started arguing with another boy and became so angry that he transformed into a wolf and killed him. Because the tribe feared the boys couldn't control themselves, they banished them to the wilderness. Wisakachek became furious when he found out about Matchitehew's mistake. He cast a new spell on him that prevented him from becoming a wolf during the day, but made him a mindless wolf at night. Keme, however, had done no wrong and was allowed to keep his transformative abilities. Fearing that Matchitehew couldn't control his abilities, though, he vanished into the forest to live on his own.

Matchitehew is now known in Native American legends as the Father of Werewolves.

Researchers working in Northern Africa during the 1930s reported on the widespread belief that people could transform into hyenas. These people, or "shapeshifters," were commonly found living in the grasslands practicing witchcraft.

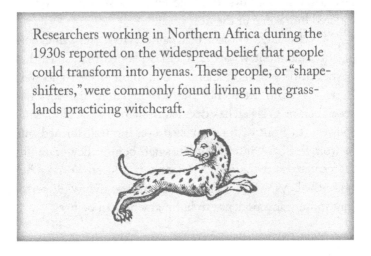

WOODLAND WEREWOLVES

One of the most popular places for werewolf sightings is Cannock Chase near Staffordshire, England. The area is very woody and features an array of hiking and mountain biking trails. In the past thirty years, there have been reports of at least twenty-one werewolf sightings. In the reports made by everyday members of the community, some witnesses say they saw a large dog that runs at incredible speed on his two hind legs. Many people insisted they saw a real werewolf, while others came up with theories of "subterranean or stone age" creatures. Whatever the theory, it's clear that this wooded area of England boasts high rates of abnormal sightings.

> If you sleep outside during a full moon, then you're likely to become a werewolf.

LONE WOLF

On August 25, 2012, *SFGate.com* posted an article about a lone wolf roaming around a large wildfire in California. Some experts thought it might be a clever strategy for picking off prey trying to escape the fire. This wolf, named Wolf OR7, gained particular interest because he was the first wolf to enter the state in nearly a century, and was being tracked using a GPS collar. He was found roaming dangerously close (within a mile to be exact) to the 63,160-acre fire that was burning out of control in Plumas County. Tracking records revealed he traveled an average of fifteen miles a day during his travels from Oregon to California. Experts reported he had an appetite for deer, despite those animals being more and more difficult to come by.

WEREWOLVES IN WISCONSIN

In 1936, one of the first werewolf sightings in Wisconsin was reported. Mark Schackelman was driving along Highway 18 when he spied a dark figure digging up an old Native American mound. As he got closer, he realized the creature stood well over six feet tall and was covered in hair. The creature had a face that resembled something between that of an ape and a dog. Schackelman noticed the creature had three human-like fingers on each hand and smelled of rotting meat.

Scared but overwhelmingly intrigued, Schackelman returned to the same spot the following night in the hopes of getting another look. This time, he was shocked not only to find the creature again, but also to hear him speak. Astounded by what he thought was a "neo-human" language, he immediately sensed the creature was evil and retreated to a safe spot to pray. After that incident, he never saw the creature again.

In 1964, a man by the name of Dennis Fewless spotted a similar creature not far from Highway 18 in Wisconsin as he was driving home from work one evening. With his headlights on, he was able to see a large animal weighing between four and five hundred pounds running across the highway. He figured the creature was at least seven feet tall and covered in coarse brown fur.

In 1972, yet another werewolf was spotted in Wisconsin. One night, a woman frantically called the police, explaining an animal was trying to break into her home. This creature was described as being nearly eight feet tall and covered in dark hair. According to the police report, it walked upright like a human and injured one of the woman's horses before trying to break into the house. When the police searched the property for clues, they found a footprint by the barn that was over a foot long. Bigfoot investigators rejected the theory that Bigfoot was behind the incident, because he'd never display such aggressive behavior, claiming instead that it must be a werewolf.

Texas Twilight

In 2010 at John Marshal High School in San Antonio, a clique started unlike any other: they were self-proclaimed werewolves. Unlike a gang looking for attention, one of the wolf pack members explained, they acted more like a family. With the popularity of movie series like *Underworld* and *Twilight* on the rise, it was understandable for teenagers to want to act out their favorite characters. Others theorized that teenagers navigating the transition from childhood to adulthood found qualities in werewolves they could relate to—perhaps not the experience of a bloodthirsty wolf, but definitely the transformational aspects. At the time,  the Northside School District counselor, Dr. Deborah Healy, said, "Young people are looking to define their identities, sometimes to come together and affiliate around a theme or an idea, just really to belong, that sense of belonging." Apparently, the wolf pack provided just that.

Teen Wolf

In the first month of 1970, teenagers from New Mexico reported seeing a werewolf wandering by the side of a road near Whitewater. When they tried to investigate, they spooked the creature and it went sprinting down the highway. Driving their car at sixty miles per hour, they could barely keep up and eventually lost the werewolf.

Henrico the Werewolf

In Virginia, there have been so many werewolf sightings that the werewolf in question has come to be known as the Werewolf of Henrico County. Since the very first sighting, the Werewolf of Henrico County has established a kind of urban legend appeal. No one seems to be able to give a first-hand account—it's always the story of a friend of a friend.

What has been said, though, is that the werewolf is grey, nearly white, and stands upright like a man. It's been rumored he walks like a tall man but has the facial features of an animal. Some say the sightings are due to a local hoax—a man dressed up in a monkey suit. However, most residents in Henrico County deny the hoax theory, saying it's possible they've mistaken a bigfoot for a werewolf. Of course, that wouldn't be the first time. Their upright statures, gargantuan feet, and furry bodies allow for human error. Without getting dangerously close to the creature, will Henrico County residents ever be able to know what he is?

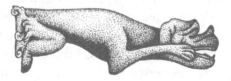

BEAST OF BRAY ROAD

The Beast of Bray Road is a cryptozoological creature that's been known to stalk the rural area of Elkhorn, Wisconsin, since the early 1980s. Some witnesses claimed to have seen the creature in other parts of Wisconsin and sometimes Illinois, but Elkhorn seems to be its favorite haunt. Bray Road itself is a quiet country highway that runs along the outskirts of Elkhorn. This is where reporter Linda Godfrey from the *Walworth County Week* newspaper went to investigate. Although she was skeptical at first, the sincerity of a witness won her over and she committed herself wholeheartedly to the investigation from then on. Her series of articles eventually became a book called *The Beast of Bray Road: Trailing Wisconsin's Werewolf.*

HEMLOCK GROVE

In 2002, a mysterious film—supposedly made in the 1970s—started getting attention. Barely over three minutes long, the film begins with what looks like simple home movies—kids riding snowmobiles, a man washing his car, etc. By the end of the film, you see the perspective of the cameraman riding his bike down a dirt road. Suddenly, he stops and zooms in on an enormous creature crouching on all fours. The camera shakes as the cameraman attempts to run away, but a few moments of rustling later, the final shot shows a flash of teeth and fangs before blacking out.

A second film was discovered soon after, and it showed police investigating the site where the previous cameraman was found dead. The camera peeks over the shoulders of two policemen observing the body, which has been torn in half by whatever creature attacked him. In an online forum discussing the films, a user identified himself as a local from the film's location. He knew a relative of the dead cameraman and said the officer was forever traumatized by what he saw. Shortly after investigating the attack, he lost his mind and kept repeating the phrase, "Dogs have four toes; bears have five."

For years after the initial discovery of the films, the debate raged online and in the media about whether they were real or not. By 2010, Steve Cook announced on History Channel's *Monster Quest* that the films were indeed fake. He claimed Mike Agrusa made both of them in 2002 and was a longtime fan of Cook's TV shows and songs. The creature in the first film was really a man in a Ghillie suit, and the dead body in the second film was simply painted Styrofoam. While Cook dramatized the investigation on *Monster Quest* to make it seem as though he discovered the flaws in the film, he later admitted to knowing about the film's phoniness before taping ever began.

Hemlock Grove is also the title of a 2013 Netflix original series about the mysterious murder of a young girl and the suspected beast that did it.

SACKED

Up until the 1980s, locals from the Iberian Peninsula were found practicing measures to keep their children from becoming werewolves. This involved having older children act as godparents to their younger siblings for fear that werewolves would recruit new members among the excess children. Also, children born with part of their amniotic sac still covering their faces were considered more susceptible to becoming werewolves.

Part Three

VAMPIRES

We don't want a thing because we have found a reason for it; we find a reason for it because we want it.

—WILL DURANT, *IMMORTAL BELOVED*

No creature, real or imagined, has ever invoked such a strong magnetic attraction as the illustrious vampire. The legendary bite on the neck invokes an immediate thrill, a sort of lust that we reserve for a passionate moment. Unlike the pathetic curse of the werewolf or the clinging screams of the banshee, the vampire life has glamour unlike most other supernatural beings. Traditionally, vampires are shockingly beautiful, and only reveal their hideous, aged nature if caught unawares whilst sleeping in their coffins.

Though most vampire legends corroborate bloodlust as a key vampire characteristic, there are actually many kinds of vampires. No one is completely immune to psychic vampirism, and in fact occult books have been dedicated to protection from psychic attacks for almost as long as the vampire stories have been put to print. Writers like Dion Fortune and Aleister Crowley knew well the nature of the psychic vampire. Modern authors such as Michele Belanger write extensively about the work of the psychic vampire—and how to act responsibly as one.

In his book *The Weiser Field Guide to Vampires*, J.M. Dixon writes:

> The fact is that many vampires blood-feed, so much so that it has become a staple in the fictions about their kind for the last several hundred years. But the commonality of it should not be considered an endorsement, nor should it be considered an excuse to practice it. Vampires are by nature intelligent and ethical creatures, and as such they believe that those who choose to

practice this method of feeding, whatever their reasons may be, do so in the most intelligent, discriminating, and clinically safe ways possible.

Today's vampire runs the full range from real to fictional. There is, of course, the famous *Twilight* series and its many vampy beasts, and HBO's *True Blood* is searingly popular. Merticus, a member of the Atlanta Vampire Alliance and a respected voice in the vampire community explains it:

> Hollywood's interpretation of the vampire has slowly begun transforming the vampire into something more human than monster. Starting with Barnabas Collins and becoming more prevalent in films such as *Interview with the Vampire* or in television shows such as HBO's *True Blood*, the humanity of the vampire has struck a chord with audiences. While these vampires aren't representative of the modern vampire community (we don't have real fangs, kill people to drink their blood, burn to a crisp in sunlight, or are required to sleep in coffins), they are indicative of some of the struggles with societal acceptance and coming to terms with who we are as a larger question of identity. While there are some in our community who enjoy living the vampire aesthetic, vampirism is largely an amalgamation of physical, mental, and in some cases spiritual attributes.

Even from a young age, I was drawn to the Addams family types, and anyone who knows me can attest to my obsession with Bela Lugosi. I loved Edward Scissorhands more than Eddie Van Halen, and central characters like Vlad Dracula (Pick me, pick me!) made my heart race. So while I am certainly offended by the misrepresentation of the creatures of the night, I am also quite guilty of fetishizing them.

One thing is certainly true, regardless of what kind of vampire you are, you want to be, or you'd like to meet—there is nothing on earth quite as appealing as a vampire story.

12

BEAUTY AND
THE PRIEST

*Sin and dandelions are very much alike. To get rid of
them is a lifetime fight, and you never quite win it.*

—William Allen White

Théophile Gautier, who wrote this story in the early 1800s
(this particular version was translated from the French version in 1908; see the next paragraph), was best known for his
work writing plays, ballets, and poetry along with historical
romance novels. A native of southwestern France, he was a
friend of Victor Hugo and spent a good deal of his life as a
journalist.

All records seem to indicate that this story was translated in 1908 by one Lafcadio Hearn. However, it appears
that Hearn died in 1904. The somewhat racy subject matter
(I'll just go ahead and say it—there is a bit of necrophilia)

must have turned a few heads in Edwardian England and America when it was translated into English in 1908. But in the lusty setting of 1836 Paris, this was no doubt a run-of-the mill form of eroticism. Clarimonde, also known as *La Morte Amoureuse*, remains a seminal work in the vampire lexicon, as well as a delicious read. Some may say this story is a lesson in temptation, others in making the correct choices in life, others in true love. I say this is a lesson in straight-up supernatural sex. The birds, the bees, and the bats in the belfry!

CLARIMONDE [LA MORTE AMOUREUSE]
by Théophile Gautier, translated from the French by Lafcadio Hearn

Brother, you ask me if I have ever loved. Yes. My story is a strange and terrible one; and though I am sixty-six years of age, I scarcely dare even now to disturb the ashes of that memory. To you I can refuse nothing; but I should not relate such a tale to any less experienced mind. So strange were the circumstances of my story, that I can scarcely believe myself to have ever actually been a party to them. For more than three years I remained the victim of a most singular and diabolical illusion. Poor country priest though I was, I led every night in a dream—would to God it had been all a dream!—a most worldly life, a damning life, a life of Sardanapalus. One single look too freely cast upon a woman well-nigh caused me to lose my soul; but finally by the grace of God and the assistance of my patron saint, I succeeded in casting out the evil spirit that possessed me. My daily life was long interwoven with a nocturnal life of a totally different character. By day I was a priest of the Lord, occupied with prayer and sacred things; by night, from the instant that I closed my eyes I became a young nobleman, a fine connoisseur in women, dogs, and horses; gambling, drinking, and blaspheming; and when I awoke at early daybreak, it seemed to me, on the other hand, that I had been sleeping, and had only dreamed that I was a priest. Of this somnambulistic life there now remains to me only the recollection of certain scenes and words which I cannot banish from my memory; but although I never actually left the walls of my presbytery, one would think to hear me speak that I were a man who, weary of all worldly pleasures, had become a religious, seeking to end a tempestuous life in the service of God, rather than a humble seminarist who has grown old in this obscure curacy, situated in the depths of the woods and even isolated from the life of the century.

Yes, I have loved as none in the world ever loved—with an insensate and furious passion—so violent that I am

astonished it did not cause my heart to burst asunder. Ah, what nights—what nights!

From my earliest childhood I had felt a vocation to the priesthood, so that all my studies were directed with that idea in view. Up to the age of twenty-four my life had been only a prolonged novitiate. Having completed my course of theology I successively received all the minor orders, and my superiors judged me worthy, despite my youth, to pass the last awful degree. My ordination was fixed for Easter week.

I had never gone into the world. My world was confined by the walls of the college and the seminary. I knew in a vague sort of a way that there was something called Woman, but I never permitted my thoughts to dwell on such a subject, and I lived in a state of perfect innocence. Twice a year only I saw my infirm and aged mother, and in those visits were comprised my sole relations with the outer world.

I regretted nothing; I felt not the least hesitation at taking the last irrevocable step; I was filled with joy and impatience. Never did a betrothed lover count the slow hours with more feverish ardour; I slept only to dream that I was saying mass; I believed there could be nothing in the world more delightful than to be a priest; I would have refused to be a king or a poet in preference. My ambition could conceive of no loftier aim.

I tell you this in order to show you that what happened to me could not have happened in the natural order of things, and to enable you to understand that I was the victim of an inexplicable fascination.

At last the great day came. I walked to the church with a step so light that I fancied myself sustained in air, or that I had wings upon my shoulders. I believed myself an angel, and wondered at the sombre and thoughtful faces of my companions, for there were several of us. I had passed all the night in prayer, and was in a condition wellnigh bordering on ecstasy. The bishop, a venerable old man, seemed to me God the Father leaning over His Eternity, and I beheld Heaven through the vault of the temple.

You well know the details of that ceremony—the benediction, the communion under both forms, the anointing of the palms of the hands with the Oil of Catechumens, and then the holy sacrifice offered in concert with the bishop.

Ah, truly spake Job when he declared that the imprudent man is one who hath not made a covenant with his eyes! I accidentally lifted my head, which until then I had kept down, and beheld before me, so close that it seemed that I could have touched her—although she was actually a considerable distance from me and on the further side of the sanctuary railing—a young woman of extraordinary beauty, and attired with royal magnificence. It seemed as though scales had suddenly fallen from my eyes. I felt like a blind man who unexpectedly recovers his sight. The bishop, so radiantly glorious but an instant before, suddenly vanished away, the tapers paled upon their golden candlesticks like stars in the dawn, and a vast darkness seemed to fill the whole church.

The charming creature appeared in bright relief against the background of that darkness, like some angelic revelation. She seemed herself radiant, and radiating light rather than receiving it.

I lowered my eyelids, firmly resolved not to again open them, that I might not be influenced by external objects, for distraction had gradually taken possession of me until I hardly knew what I was doing.

In another minute, nevertheless, I reopened my eyes, for through my eyelashes I still beheld her, all sparkling with prismatic colours, and surrounded with such a penumbra as one beholds in gazing at the sun.

Oh, how beautiful she was! The greatest painters, who followed ideal beauty into heaven itself, and thence brought back to earth the true portrait of the Madonna, never in their delineations even approached that wildly beautiful reality which I saw before me. Neither the verses of the poet nor the palette of the artist could convey any conception of her. She was rather tall, with a form and bearing of a goddess. Her hair, of a soft blonde hue, was parted in the midst and flowed back over her temples in two rivers of rippling gold; she seemed a diademed queen. Her forehead, bluish-white in its transparency, extended its calm breadth above the arches of her eyebrows, which by a strange singularity were almost black, and admirably relieved the effect of sea-green eyes of unsustainable vivacity and brilliancy. What eyes! With a single flash they could have decided a man's destiny. They had a life, a limpidity, an ardour, a humid light which I have never seen in human eyes; they shot forth rays like arrows, which I could distinctly *see* enter my heart. I know not if the fire which illumined them came from heaven or from hell, but assuredly it came from one or the other. That woman was either an angel or a demon, perhaps both. Assuredly she never sprang from the flank of Eve, our common mother. Teeth of the most lustrous pearl gleamed in her ruddy smile, and at every inflection of her lips little dimples appeared in the satiny rose of her adorable cheeks. There was a delicacy and pride in the regal outline of her nostrils bespeaking noble blood. Agate gleams played over the smooth lustrous skin of her half-bare shoulders, and strings of great blonde pearls—almost equal to her neck in beauty of colour—descended upon her bosom. From time to time she elevated her head with the undulating grace of a startled serpent or peacock, thereby imparting a quivering motion to the high lace ruff which surrounded it like a silver trellis-work.

What eyes! With a single flash they could have decided a man's destiny. They had a life, a limpidity, an ardour, a humid light which I have never seen in human eyes; they shot forth rays like arrows, which I could distinctly see *enter my heart.*

She wore a robe of orange-red velvet, and from her wide ermine-lined sleeves there peeped forth patrician hands of infinite delicacy, and so ideally transparent that, like the fingers of Aurora, they permitted the light to shine through them.

All these details I can recollect at this moment as plainly as though they were of yesterday, for notwithstanding I was greatly troubled at the time, nothing escaped me; the faintest touch of shading, the little dark speck at the point of the chin, the imperceptible down at the corners of the lips, the velvety floss upon the brow, the quivering shadows of the eyelashes upon the cheeks—I could notice everything with astonishing lucidity of perception.

And gazing I felt opening within me gates that had until then remained closed; vents long obstructed became all clear, permitting glimpses of unfamiliar perspectives within; life suddenly made itself visible to me under a totally novel aspect. I felt as though I had just been born into a new world and a new order of things. A frightful anguish commenced to torture my heart as with red-hot pincers. Every successive minute seemed to me at once but a second and yet a century. Meanwhile the ceremony was proceeding, and I shortly found myself transported far from that world of which my newly born desires were furiously besieging the entrance. Nevertheless I answered 'Yes' when I wished to say 'No,' though all within me protested against the violence done to my soul by my tongue. Some occult power seemed to force the words from my throat against my will. Thus it is, perhaps, that so many young girls walk to the altar firmly resolved to refuse in a startling manner the husband imposed upon them, and that yet not one ever fulfills her intention. Thus it is, doubtless, that so many poor novices take the veil, though they have resolved to tear it into shreds at the moment when called upon to utter the vows. One dares not thus cause so great a scandal to all present, nor deceive the expectation of so many people. All those eyes, all those wills seem to weigh down upon you like a cope of lead, and, moreover, measures have been so well taken, everything has been so thoroughly arranged beforehand and after a fashion so evidently irrevocable, that the will yields to the weight of circumstances and utterly breaks down.

As the ceremony proceeded the features of the fair unknown changed their expression. Her look had at first been one of caressing tenderness; it changed to an air of disdain and of mortification, as though at not having been able to make itself understood.

With an effort of will sufficient to have uprooted a mountain, I strove to cry out that I would not be a priest, but I could not speak; my tongue seemed nailed to my palate, and I found it impossible to express my will by the least syllable of negation. Though fully awake, I felt like one under the influence of a nightmare, who vainly strives to shriek out the one word upon which life depends.

She seemed conscious of the martyrdom I was undergoing, and, as though to encourage me, she gave me a look replete with divinest promise. Her eyes were a poem; their every glance was a song.

She said to me:

'If thou wilt be mine, I shall make thee happier than God Himself in His paradise. The angels themselves will be jealous of thee. Tear off that funeral shroud in which thou art about to wrap thyself. I am Beauty, I am Youth, I am Life. Come to me! Together we shall be Love. Can Jehovah offer thee aught in exchange? Our lives will flow on like a dream, in one eternal kiss.

'Fling forth the wine of that chalice, and thou art free. I will conduct thee to the Unknown Isles. Thou shalt sleep in my bosom upon a bed of massy gold under a silver pavilion, for I love thee and would take thee away from thy God, before whom so many noble hearts pour forth floods of love which never reach even the steps of His throne!'

These words seemed to float to my ears in a rhythm of infinite sweetness, for her look was actually sonorous, and the utterances of her eyes were reechoed in the depths of my heart as though living lips had breathed them into my life. I felt myself willing to renounce God, and yet my tongue mechanically fulfilled all the formalities of the ceremony. The fair one gave me another look, so beseeching, so despairing that keen blades seemed to pierce my heart, and I felt my bosom transfixed by more swords than those of Our Lady of Sorrows.

All was consummated; I had become a priest.

Never was deeper anguish painted on human face than upon hers. The maiden who beholds her affianced lover suddenly fall dead at her side, the mother bending over the empty cradle of her child, Eve seated at the threshold of the gate of Paradise, the miser who finds a stone substituted for his stolen treasure, the poet who accidentally permits the only manuscript of his finest work to fall into the fire, could not wear a look so despairing, so inconsolable. All the blood had abandoned her charming face, leaving it whiter than marble; her beautiful arms hung lifelessly on either side of her body as though their muscles had suddenly relaxed, and she sought the support of a pillar, for her yielding limbs almost betrayed her. As for myself, I staggered toward the door of the church, livid as death, my forehead bathed with a sweat bloodier than that of Calvary; I felt as though I were being strangled; the vault seemed to have flattened down upon my shoulders, and it seemed to me that my head alone sustained the whole weight of the dome.

As I was about to cross the threshold a hand suddenly caught mine—a woman's hand! I had never till then touched the hand of any woman. It was cold as a serpent's skin, and yet its impress remained upon my wrist, burnt there as though branded by a glowing iron. It was she. 'Unhappy man! Unhappy man! What hast thou done?' she exclaimed in a low voice, and immediately disappeared in the crowd.

The aged bishop passed by. He cast a severe and scrutinising look upon me. My face presented the wildest aspect imaginable: I blushed and turned pale alternately; dazzling lights flashed before my eyes. A companion took pity on me. He seized my arm and led me out. I could not

It was cold as a serpent's skin, and yet its impress remained upon my wrist, burnt there as though branded by a glowing iron.

possibly have found my way back to the seminary unassisted. At the corner of a street, while the young priest's attention was momentarily turned in another direction, a negro page, fantastically garbed, approached me, and without pausing on his way slipped into my hand a little pocket-book with gold-embroidered corners, at the same time giving me a sign to hide it. I concealed it in my sleeve, and there kept it until I found myself alone in my cell. Then I opened the clasp. There were only two leaves within, bearing the words, 'Clarimonde. At the Concini Palace.' So little acquainted was I at that time with the things of this world that I had never heard of Clarimonde, celebrated as she was, and I had no idea as to where the Concini Palace was situated. I hazarded a thousand conjectures, each more extravagant than the last; but, in truth, I cared little whether she were a great lady or a courtesan, so that I could but see her once more.

My love, although the growth of a single hour, had taken imperishable root. I did not even dream of attempting to tear it up, so fully was I convinced such a thing would be impossible. That woman had completely taken possession of me. One look from her had sufficed to change my very nature. She had breathed her will into my life, and I no longer lived in myself, but in her and for her. I gave myself up to a thousand extravagancies. I kissed the place upon my hand which she had touched, and I repeated her name over and over again for hours in succession. I only needed to close my eyes in order to see her distinctly as though she were actually present; and I reiterated to myself the words she had uttered in my ear at the church porch: 'Unhappy man! Unhappy man! What hast thou done?' I comprehended at last the full horror of my situation, and the funereal and awful restraints of the state into which I had just entered became clearly revealed to me. To be a priest!—that is, to be chaste, to never love, to observe no distinction of sex or age, to turn from the sight of all beauty, to put out one's own eyes, to hide for ever crouching in the chill shadows of some church or cloister, to visit none but the dying, to watch by unknown corpses, and ever bear about with one the black soutane as a garb of mourning for oneself, so that your very dress might serve as a pall for your coffin.

And I felt life rising within me like a subterranean lake, expanding and overflowing; my blood leaped fiercely through my arteries; my long-restrained youth suddenly burst into active being, like the aloe which blooms but once in a hundred years, and then bursts into blossom with a clap of thunder.

What could I do in order to see Clarimonde once more? I had no pretext to offer for desiring to leave the seminary, not knowing any person in the city. I would not even be able to remain there but a short time, and was only waiting my

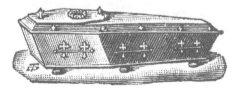

assignment to the curacy which I must thereafter occupy. I tried to remove the bars of the window; but it was at a fearful height from the ground, and I found that as I had no ladder it would be useless to think of escaping thus. And, furthermore, I could descend thence only by night in any event, and afterward how should I be able to find my way through the inextricable labyrinth of streets? All these difficulties, which to many would have appeared altogether insignificant, were gigantic to me, a poor seminarist who had fallen in love only the day before for the first time, without experience, without money, without attire.

'Ah!' cried I to myself in my blindness, 'were I not a priest I could have seen her every day; I might have been her lover, her spouse. Instead of being wrapped in this dismal shroud of mine I would have had garments of silk and velvet, golden chains, a sword, and fair plumes like other handsome young cavaliers. My hair, instead of being dishonoured by the tonsure, would flow down upon my neck in waving curls; I would have a fine waxed moustache; I would be a gallant.' But one hour passed before an altar, a few hastily articulated words, had for ever cut me off from the number of the living, and I had myself sealed down the stone

of my own tomb; I had with my own hand bolted the gate of my prison! I went to the window. The sky was beautifully blue; the trees had donned their spring robes; nature seemed to be making parade of an ironical joy. The *Place* was filled with people, some going, others coming; young beaux and young beauties were sauntering in couples toward the groves and gardens; merry youths passed by, cheerily trolling refrains of drinking-songs—it was all a picture of vivacity, life, animation, gaiety, which formed a bitter contrast with my mourning and my solitude. On the steps of the gate sat a young mother playing with her child. She kissed its little rosy mouth still impearled with drops of milk, and performed, in order to amuse it, a thousand divine little puerilities such as only mothers know how to invent. The father standing at a little distance smiled gently upon the charming group, and with folded arms seemed to hug his joy to his heart. I could not endure that spectacle. I closed the window with violence, and flung myself on my bed, my heart filled with frightful hate and jealousy, and gnawed my fingers and my bedcovers like a tiger that has passed ten days without food.

I know not how long I remained in this condition, but at last, while writhing on the bed in a fit of spasmodic fury, I suddenly perceived the Abbé Sérapion, who was standing erect in the centre of the room, watching me attentively. Filled with shame of myself, I let my head fall upon my breast and covered my face with my hands.

'Romuald, my friend, something very extraordinary is transpiring within you,' observed Sérapion, after a few moments' silence; 'your conduct is altogether inexplicable. You—always so quiet, so pious, so gentle—you to rage in your cell like a wild beast! Take heed, brother—do not listen to the suggestions of the devil The Evil Spirit, furious that you have consecrated yourself for ever to the Lord, is prowling around you like a ravening wolf and making a last effort to obtain possession of you. Instead of allowing yourself to be conquered, my dear Romuald, make to yourself a cuirass of prayers, a buckler of mortifications, and combat the enemy like a valiant man; you will then assuredly overcome him. Virtue must be proved by temptation, and gold comes forth purer from the hands of the assayer. Fear not. Never allow yourself to become discouraged. The most watchful and steadfast souls are at moments liable to such temptation. Pray, fast, meditate, and the Evil Spirit will depart from you.'

The words of the Abbé Sérapion restored me to myself, and I became a little more calm. 'I came,' he continued, 'to tell you that you have been appointed to the curacy of C———. The priest who had charge of it has just died, and Monseigneur the Bishop has ordered me to have you installed there at once. Be ready, therefore, to start to-morrow.' I responded with an inclination of the head, and the Abbé retired. I opened my missal and commenced reading some prayers, but the letters became confused and blurred under my eyes, the thread of the ideas entangled itself hopelessly in my brain, and the volume at last fell from my hands without my being aware of it.

To leave to-morrow without having been able to see her again, to add yet another barrier to the many already interposed between us, to lose for ever all hope of being able to meet her, except, indeed, through a miracle! Even to write to her, alas! would be impossible, for by whom could I dispatch my letter? With my sacred character of priest, to whom could I dare unbosom myself, in whom could I confide? I became a prey to the bitterest anxiety.

Then suddenly recurred to me the words of the Abbé Sérapion regarding the artifices of the devil; and the strange character of the adventure, the supernatural beauty of Clarimonde, the phosphoric light of her eyes, the burning imprint of her hand, the agony into which she had thrown me, the sudden change wrought within me when all my piety vanished in a single instant—these and other things clearly testified to the work of the Evil One, and perhaps that satiny hand was but the glove which concealed his claws. Filled with terror at these fancies, I again picked up the missal which had slipped from my knees and fallen upon the floor, and once more gave myself up to prayer.

Next morning Sérapion came to take me away. Two mules freighted with our miserable valises awaited us at the gate. He mounted one, and I the other as well as I knew how.

As we passed along the streets of the city, I gazed attentively at all the windows and balconies in the hope of seeing Clarimonde, but it was yet early in the morning, and the city had hardly opened its eyes. Mine sought to penetrate the blinds and window-curtains of all the palaces before which we were passing. Sérapion doubtless attributed this curiosity to my admiration of the architecture, for he slackened the pace of his animal in order to give me time to look around me. At last we passed the city gates and commenced to mount the hill beyond. When we arrived at its summit I turned to take a last look at the place where Clarimonde dwelt. The shadow of a great cloud hung over all the city; the contrasting colours of its blue and red roofs were lost in the uniform half-tint, through which here and there floated upward, like white flakes of foam, the smoke of freshly kindled fires. By a singular optical effect one edifice, which surpassed in height all the neighbouring buildings that were still dimly veiled by the vapours, towered up, fair and lustrous with the gilding of a solitary beam of sunlight—although actually more than a league away it seemed quite near. The smallest details of its architecture were plainly distinguishable—the turrets, the platforms, the window-casements, and even the swallow-tailed weather-vanes.

'What is that palace I see over there, all lighted up by the sun?' I asked Sérapion. He shaded his eyes with his hand, and having looked in the direction indicated, replied: 'It is the ancient palace which the Prince Concini has given to the courtesan Clarimonde. Awful things are done there!'

At that instant, I know not yet whether it was a reality or an illusion, I fancied I saw gliding along the terrace a shapely white figure, which gleamed for a moment in passing and as quickly vanished. It was Clarimonde.

Oh, did she know that at that very hour, all feverish and restless—from the height of the rugged road which separated me from her, and which, alas! I could never more descend—I was directing my eyes upon the palace where she dwelt, and which a mocking beam of sunlight seemed to bring nigh to me, as though inviting me to enter therein as its lord? Undoubtedly she must have known it, for her soul was too sympathetically united with mine not to have felt its least emotional thrill, and that subtle sympathy it must have been which prompted her to climb—although clad only in her nightdress—to the summit of the terrace, amid the icy dews of the morning.

I fancied I saw gliding along the terrace a shapely white figure, which gleamed for a moment in passing and as quickly vanished.

The shadow gained the palace, and the scene became to the eye only a motionless ocean of roofs and gables, amid which one mountainous undulation was distinctly visible. Sérapion urged his mule forward, my own at once followed at the same gait, and a sharp angle in the road at last hid the city of S——— for ever from my eyes, as I was destined never to return thither. At the close of a weary three-days' journey through dismal country fields, we caught sight of the cock upon the steeple of the church which I was to take charge of, peeping above the trees, and after having followed some winding roads fringed with thatched cottages and little gardens, we found ourselves in front of the façade, which certainly possessed few features of magnificence. A porch ornamented with some mouldings, and two or three pillars rudely hewn from sandstone; a tiled roof with counterforts of the same sandstone as the pillars—that was all. To the left lay the cemetery, overgrown with high weeds, and having a great iron cross rising up in its centre; to the right stood the presbytery under the shadow of the church. It was a house of the most extreme simplicity and frigid cleanliness. We entered the enclosure. A few chickens were picking up some oats scattered upon the ground; accustomed, seemingly, to the black habit of ecclesiastics, they showed no fear of our presence and scarcely troubled themselves to get out of our way. A hoarse, wheezy barking fell upon our ears, and we saw an aged dog running toward us.

It was my predecessor's dog. He had dull bleared eyes, grizzled hair, and every mark of the greatest age to which a dog can possibly attain. I patted him gently, and he proceeded at once to march along beside me with an air of satisfaction unspeakable. A very old woman, who had been the housekeeper of the former curé, also came to meet us, and after having invited me into a little back parlour, asked whether I intended to retain her. I replied that I would take care of her, and the dog, and the chickens, and all the furniture her master had bequeathed her at his death. At this she became fairly transported with joy, and the Abbé Sérapion at once paid her the price which she asked for her little property.

As soon as my installation was over, the Abbé Sérapion returned to the seminary. I was, therefore, left alone, with no one but myself to look to for aid or counsel. The thought of Clarimonde again began to haunt me, and in spite of all my endeavours to banish it, I always found it present in my meditations. One evening, while promenading in my little garden along the walks bordered with box-plants, I fancied that I saw through the elm-trees the figure of a woman, who followed my every movement, and that I beheld two sea-green eyes gleaming through the foliage; but it was only an illusion, and on going round to the other side of the garden, I could find nothing except a footprint on the sanded walk—a footprint so small that it seemed to have been made by the foot of a child. The garden was enclosed by very high walls. I searched every nook and corner of it, but could discover no one there. I have never succeeded in fully accounting for this circumstance, which, after all, was nothing compared with the strange things which happened to me afterward.

For a whole year I lived thus, filling all the duties of my calling with the most scrupulous exactitude, praying and fasting, exhorting and lending ghostly aid to the sick, and bestowing alms even to the extent of frequently depriving myself of the very necessaries of life. But I felt a great aridness within me, and the sources of grace seemed closed against me. I never found that happiness which should spring from the fulfilment of a holy mission; my thoughts were far away, and the words of Clarimonde were ever upon my lips like an involuntary refrain. Oh, brother, meditate well on this! Through having but once lifted my eyes to look upon a woman, through one fault apparently so venial, I have for years remained a victim to the most miserable agonies, and the happiness of my life has been destroyed for ever.

I will not longer dwell upon those defeats, or on those inward victories invariably followed by yet more terrible falls, but will at once proceed to the facts of my story. One night my door-bell was long and violently rung. The aged housekeeper arose and opened to the stranger, and the figure of a man, whose complexion was deeply bronzed, and who was richly clad in a foreign costume, with a poniard at his girdle, appeared under the rays of Barbara's lantern. Her first impulse was one of terror, but the stranger reassured her, and stated that he desired to see me at once on matters relating to my holy calling. Barbara invited him upstairs, where I was on the point of retiring. The stranger told me that his mistress, a very noble lady, was lying at the point of death, and desired to see a priest. I replied that I was prepared to follow him, took with me the sacred articles necessary for extreme unction, and descended in all haste. Two horses black as the night itself stood without the gate, pawing the ground with impatience, and veiling their chests with long streams of smoky vapour exhaled from their nostrils. He held the stirrup and aided me to mount upon one;

then, merely laying his hand upon the pommel of the saddle, he vaulted on the other, pressed the animal's sides with his knees, and loosened rein. The horse bounded forward with the velocity of an arrow. Mine, of which the stranger held the bridle, also started off at a swift gallop, keeping up with his companion. We devoured the road. The ground flowed backward beneath us in a long streaked line of pale gray, and the black silhouettes of the trees seemed fleeing by us on either side like an army in rout. We passed through a forest so profoundly gloomy that I felt my flesh creep in the chill darkness with superstitious fear. The showers of bright sparks which flew from the stony road under the ironshod feet of our horses remained glowing in our wake like a fiery trail; and had any one at that hour of the night beheld us both—my guide and myself—he must have taken us for two spectres riding upon nightmares. Witch-fires ever and anon flitted across the road before us, and the night-birds shrieked fearsomely in the depth of the woods beyond, where we beheld at intervals glow the phosphorescent eyes of wild cats. The manes of the horses became more and more dishevelled, the sweat streamed over their flanks, and their breath came through their nostrils hard and fast. But when he found them slacking pace, the guide reanimated them by uttering a strange, guttural, unearthly cry, and the gallop recommenced with fury. At last the whirlwind race ceased; a huge black mass pierced through with many bright points of light suddenly rose before us, the hoofs of our horses echoed louder upon a strong wooden drawbridge, and we rode under a great vaulted archway which darkly yawned between two enormous towers. Some great excitement evidently reigned in the castle. Servants with torches were crossing the court-yard in every direction, and above lights were ascending and descending from landing to landing. I obtained a confused glimpse of vast masses of architecture—columns, arcades, flights of steps, stairways—a royal voluptuousness and elfin magnificence of construction worthy of fairyland. A negro page—the same who had before brought me the tablet from Clarimonde, and whom I instantly recognised—approached to aid me in dismounting, and the major-domo, attired in black velvet with a gold chain about his neck, advanced to meet me, supporting himself upon an ivory cane. Large tears were falling from his eyes and streaming over his cheeks and white beard. 'Too late!' he cried, sorrowfully shaking his

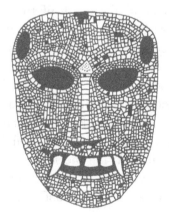

venerable head. 'Too late, sir priest! But if you have not been able to save the soul, come at least to watch by the poor body.'

He took my arm and conducted me to the death-chamber. I wept not less bitterly than he, for I had learned that the dead one was none other than that Clarimonde whom I had so deeply and so wildly loved. A *prie-dieu* stood at the foot of the bed; a bluish flame flickering in a bronze pattern filled all the room with a wan, deceptive light, here and there bringing out in the darkness at intervals some projection of furniture or cornice. In a chiseled urn upon the table there was a faded white rose, whose leaves—excepting one that still held—had all fallen, like odorous tears, to the foot of the vase. A broken black mask, a fan, and disguises of every variety, which were lying on the armchairs, bore witness that death had entered suddenly and unannounced into that sumptuous dwelling. Without daring to cast my eyes upon the bed, I knelt down and commenced to repeat the Psalms for the Dead, with exceeding fervour, thanking God that He had placed the tomb between me and the memory of this woman, so that I might thereafter be able to utter her name in my prayers as a name for ever sanctified by death. But my fervour gradually weakened, and I fell insensibly into a reverie. That chamber bore no semblance to a chamber of death. In lieu of the fetid and cadaverous odours which I had been accustomed to breathe during such funereal vigils, a languorous vapour of Oriental perfume—I know not what amorous odour of woman—softly floated through the tepid air. That pale light seemed rather a twilight gloom contrived for voluptuous pleasure, than a substitute for the yellow-flickering watch-tapers which shine by the side of corpses. I thought upon the strange destiny which enabled me to meet Clarimonde again at the very moment when she was lost to me for ever, and a sigh of regretful anguish escaped from my breast. Then it seemed to me that some one behind me had also sighed, and I turned round to look. It was only an echo. But in that moment my eyes fell upon the bed of death which they had till then avoided. The red damask curtains, decorated with large flowers worked in embroidery and looped up with gold bullion, permitted me to behold the fair dead, lying at full length, with hands joined upon her bosom. She was covered with a linen wrapping of dazzling whiteness, which formed a strong contrast with the gloomy purple of the hangings, and was of so fine a texture that it concealed nothing of her body's charming form, and allowed the eye to follow those beautiful outlines—undulating like the neck of a swan—which even death had not robbed of their supple grace. She seemed an alabaster statue executed by some skillful sculptor to place upon the tomb of a queen, or rather, perhaps, like a slumbering maiden over whom the silent snow had woven a spotless veil.

I could no longer maintain my constrained attitude of prayer. The air of the alcove intoxicated me, that febrile perfume of half-faded roses penetrated my very brain, and I commenced to pace restlessly up and down the chamber, pausing at each turn before the bier to contemplate the graceful corpse lying beneath the transparency of its shroud.

Wild fancies came thronging to my brain. I thought to myself that she might not, perhaps, be really dead; that she might only have feigned death for the purpose of bringing me to her castle, and then declaring her love. At one time I even thought I saw her foot move under the whiteness of the coverings, and slightly disarrange the long straight folds of the winding-sheet.

And then I asked myself: 'Is this indeed Clarimonde? What proof have I that it is she? Might not that black page have passed into the service of some other lady? Surely, I must be going mad to torture and afflict myself thus!' But my heart answered with a fierce throbbing: 'It is she; it is she indeed!' I approached the bed again, and fixed my eyes with redoubled attention upon the object of my incertitude. Ah, must I confess it? That exquisite perfection of bodily form, although purified and made sacred by the shadow of death, affected me more voluptuously than it should have done; and that repose so closely resembled slumber that one might well have mistaken it for such. I forgot that I had come there to perform a funeral ceremony; I fancied myself a young bridegroom entering the chamber of the bride, who all modestly hides her fair face, and through coyness seeks to keep herself wholly veiled. Heartbroken with grief, yet

She seemed an alabaster statue executed by some skillful sculptor to place upon the tomb of a queen, or rather, perhaps, like a slumbering maiden over whom the silent snow had woven a spotless veil.

wild with hope, shuddering at once with fear and pleasure, I bent over her and grasped the corner of the sheet. I lifted it back, holding my breath all the while through fear of waking her. My arteries throbbed with such violence that I felt them hiss through my temples, and the sweat poured from my forehead in streams, as though I had lifted a mighty slab of marble. There, indeed, lay Clarimonde, even as I had seen her at the church on the day of my ordination. She was not less charming than then. With her, death seemed but a last coquetry. The pallor of her cheeks, the less brilliant carnation of her lips, her long eyelashes lowered and relieving their dark fringe against that white skin, lent her an unspeakably seductive aspect of melancholy chastity and mental suffering; her long loose hair, still intertwined with some little blue flowers, made a shining pillow for her head, and veiled the nudity of her shoulders with its thick ringlets; her beautiful hands, purer, more diaphanous, than the Host, were crossed on her bosom in an attitude of pious rest and silent prayer, which served to counteract all that might have proven otherwise too alluring—even after death—in the exquisite roundness and ivory polish of her bare arms from which the pearl bracelets had not yet been removed. I remained long in mute contemplation, and the more I gazed, the less could I persuade myself that life had really abandoned that beautiful body for ever. I do not know whether it was an illusion or a reflection of the lamplight, but it seemed to me that the blood was again commencing to circulate under that lifeless pallor, although she remained all motionless. I laid my hand lightly on her arm; it was cold, but not colder than her hand on the day when it touched mine at the portals of the church. I resumed my position, bending my face above her, and bathing her cheek with the warm dew of my tears. Ah, what bitter feelings of despair and helplessness, what agonies unutterable did I endure in that long watch! Vainly did I wish that I could have gathered all my life into one mass that I might give it all to her, and breathe into her chill remains the flame which devoured me. The night advanced, and feeling the moment of eternal separation approach, I could not deny myself the last sad sweet pleasure of imprinting a kiss upon the dead lips of her who had been my only love . . . Oh, miracle! A faint breath mingled itself with my breath, and the mouth of Clarimonde responded to the passionate pressure of mine. Her eyes unclosed, and lighted up with something of their former brilliancy; she uttered a long sigh, and uncrossing her arms, passed them around my neck with a look of ineffable delight. 'Ah, it is thou, Romuald!' she murmured in a voice languishingly sweet as the last vibrations of

a harp. 'What ailed thee, dearest? I waited so long for thee that I am dead; but we are now betrothed: I can see thee and visit thee. Adieu, Romuald, adieu! I love thee. That is all I wished to tell thee, and I give thee back the life which thy kiss for a moment recalled. We shall soon meet again.'

Her head fell back, but her arms yet encircled me, as though to retain me still. A furious whirlwind suddenly burst in the window, and entered the chamber. The last remaining leaf of the white rose for a moment palpitated at the extremity of the stalk like a butterfly's wing, then it detached itself and flew forth through the open casement, bearing with it the soul of Clarimonde. The lamp was extinguished, and I fell insensible upon the bosom of the beautiful dead.

When I came to myself again I was lying on the bed in my little room at the presbytery, and the old dog of the former curé was licking my hand, which had been hanging down outside of the covers. Barbara, all trembling with age and anxiety, was busying herself about the room, opening and shutting drawers, and emptying powders into glasses. On seeing me open my eyes, the old woman uttered a cry of joy, the dog yelped and wagged his tail, but I was still so weak that I could not speak a single word or make the slightest motion. Afterward I learned that I had lain thus for three days, giving no evidence of

> *Vainly did I wish that I could have gathered all my life into one mass that I might give it all to her, and breathe into her chill remains the flame which devoured me.*

life beyond the faintest respiration. Those three days do not reckon in my life, nor could I ever imagine whither my spirit had departed during those three days; I have no recollection of aught relating to them. Barbara told me that the same coppery-complexioned man who came to seek me on the night of my departure from the presbytery had brought me back the next morning in a close litter, and departed immediately afterward. When I became able to collect my scattered thoughts, I reviewed within my mind all the circumstances of that fateful night. At first I thought I had been the victim of some magical illusion, but ere long the recollection of other circumstances, real and palpable in themselves, came to forbid that supposition. I could not believe that I had been dreaming, since Barbara as well as myself had seen the strange man with his two black horses, and described with exactness every detail of his figure and apparel. Nevertheless it appeared that none knew of any castle in the neighbourhood answering to the description of that in which I had again found Clarimonde. One morning I found the Abbé Sérapion in my room. Barbara had advised him that I was ill, and he had come with all speed to see me. Although this haste on his part testified to an affectionate interest in me, yet his visit did not cause me the pleasure which it should have done. The Abbé Sérapion had something penetrating and inquisitorial in his gaze which made me feel very ill at ease. His presence filled me with embarrassment and a sense of guilt. At the first glance he divined my interior trouble, and I hated him for his clairvoyance. While he inquired after

my health in hypocritically honeyed accents, he constantly kept his two great yellow lion-eyes fixed upon me, and
plunged his look into my soul like a sounding-lead. Then he
asked me how I directed my parish, if I was happy in it, how I
passed the leisure hours allowed me in the intervals of pasto-
ral duty, whether I had become acquainted with many of the
inhabitants of the place, what was my favourite reading, and
a thousand other such questions. I answered these inquiries
as briefly as possible, and he, without ever waiting for my
answers, passed rapidly from one subject of query to another.
That conversation had evidently no connection with what he
actually wished to say. At last, without any premonition, but
as though repeating a piece of news which he had recalled on
the instant, and feared might otherwise be forgotten subsequently, he suddenly said, in a clear vibrant voice, which rang
in my ears like the trumpets of the Last Judgment:

'The great courtesan Clarimonde died a few days ago, at
the close of an orgie which lasted eight
days and eight nights. It was something infernally splendid. The abomi-
nations of the banquets of Belshaz-
zar and Cleopatra were re-enacted
there. Good God, what age are we
living in? The guests were served by swarthy slaves who spoke an unknown tongue,
and who seemed to me to be veritable
demons. The livery of the very least

among them would have served for the gala-dress of an emperor. There have always been very strange stories told of this Clarimonde, and all her lovers came to a violent or miserable end. They used to say that she was a ghoul, a female vampire; but I believe she was none other than Beelzebub himself.'

He ceased to speak, and commenced to regard me more attentively than ever, as though to observe the effect of his words on me. I could not refrain from starting when I heard him utter the name of Clarimonde, and this news of her death, in addition to the pain it caused me by reason of its coincidence with the nocturnal scenes I had witnessed, filled me with an agony and terror which my face betrayed, despite my utmost endeavours to appear composed. Sérapion fixed an anxious and severe look upon me, and then observed: 'My son, I must warn you that you are standing with foot raised upon the brink of an abyss; take heed lest you fall therein. Satan's claws are long, and tombs are not always true to their trust. The tombstone of Clarimonde should be sealed down with a triple seal, for, if report be true, it is not the first time she has died. May God watch over you, Romuald!'

There have always been very strange stories told of this Clarimonde, and all her lovers came to a violent or miserable end.

And with these words the Abbé walked slowly to the door. I did not see him again at that time, for he left for S——— almost immediately.

I became completely restored to health and resumed my accustomed duties. The memory of Clarimonde and the words of the old Abbé were constantly in my mind; nevertheless no extraordinary event had occurred to verify the funereal predictions of Sérapion, and I had commenced to believe that his fears and my own terrors were over-exaggerated, when one night I had a strange dream. I had hardly fallen asleep when I heard my bed-curtains drawn apart, as their rings slided back upon the curtain rod with a sharp sound. I rose up quickly upon my elbow, and beheld the shadow of a woman standing erect before me. I recognised Clarimonde immediately. She bore in her hand a little lamp, shaped like those which are placed in tombs, and its light lent her fingers a rosy transparency, which extended itself by lessening degrees even to the opaque and milky whiteness of her bare arm. Her only garment was the linen winding-sheet which had shrouded her when lying upon the bed of death. She sought to gather its folds over her bosom as though ashamed of being so scantily clad, but her little hand was not equal to the task. She was so white that the colour of the drapery blended with that of her flesh under the pallid rays of the lamp. Enveloped with this subtle tissue which betrayed all the contour of her body, she seemed

rather the marble statue of some fair antique bather than a woman endowed with life. But dead or living, statue or woman, shadow or body, her beauty was still the same, only that the green light of her eyes was less brilliant, and her mouth, once so warmly crimson, was only tinted with a faint tender rosiness, like that of her cheeks. The little blue flowers which I had noticed entwined in her hair were withered and dry, and had lost nearly all their leaves, but this did not prevent her from being charming—so charming that, notwithstanding the strange character of the adventure, and the unexplainable manner in which she had entered my room, I felt not even for a moment the least fear.

She placed the lamp on the table and seated herself at the foot of my bed; then bending toward me, she said, in that voice at once silvery clear and yet velvety in its sweet softness, such as I never heard from any lips save hers:

'I have kept thee long in waiting, dear Romuald, and it must have seemed to thee that I had forgotten thee. But I come from afar off, very far off, and from a land whence no other has ever yet returned. There is neither sun nor moon in that land whence I come: all is but space and shadow; there is neither road nor pathway: no earth for the foot, no air for the wing; and nevertheless behold me here, for Love is stronger than Death and must conquer him in the end. Oh what sad faces and fearful things I have seen on my way hither! What difficulty my soul, returned to earth through the power of will alone, has had in finding its body and reinstating itself therein! What terrible efforts I had to make ere I could lift the ponderous slab with which they had covered me! See, the palms of my poor hands are all bruised! Kiss them, sweet love, that they may be healed!' She laid the cold palms of her hands upon my mouth, one after the other. I kissed them, indeed, many times, and she the while watched me with a smile of ineffable affection.

I confess to my shame that I had entirely forgotten the advice of the Abbé Sérapion and the sacred office wherewith I had been invested. I had fallen without resistance, and at the first assault. I had not even made the least effort to repel the tempter. The fresh coolness of Clarimonde's skin penetrated my own, and I felt voluptuous tremors pass over my whole body. Poor child! in spite of all I saw afterward, I can hardly yet believe she was a demon; at least she had no appearance of being such, and never did Satan so skillfully conceal his claws and horns. She had drawn her feet up beneath her, and squatted down on the edge of the couch in an attitude full of negligent coquetry. From time to time she passed her little hand through my hair and twisted it into curls, as though trying how a new style of wearing it would become my face. I abandoned myself to her hands with the most guilty pleasure, while she accompanied her gentle play with the prettiest prattle. The most remarkable fact

> *In spite of all I saw afterward, I can hardly yet believe she was a demon; at least she had no appearance of being such, and never did Satan so skillfully conceal his claws and horns.*

was that I felt no astonishment whatever at so extraordinary an adventure, and as in dreams one finds no difficulty in accepting the most fantastic events as simple facts, so all these circumstances seemed to me perfectly natural in themselves.

'I loved thee long ere I saw thee, dear Romuald, and sought thee everywhere. Thou wast my dream, and I first saw thee in the church at the fatal moment. I said at once, "It is he!" I gave thee a look into which I threw all the love I ever had, all the love I now have, all the love I shall ever have for thee—a look that would have damned a cardinal or brought a king to his knees at my feet in view of all his court. Thou remainedst unmoved, preferring thy God to me!

'Ah, how jealous I am of that God whom thou didst love and still lovest more than me!

'Woe is me, unhappy one that I am! I can never have thy heart all to myself, I whom thou didst recall to life with a kiss—dead Clarimonde, who for thy sake bursts asunder the gates of the tomb, and comes to consecrate to thee a life which she has resumed only to make thee happy!'

All her words were accompanied with the most impassioned caresses, which bewildered my sense and my reason to such an extent, that I did not fear to utter a frightful blasphemy for the sake of consoling her, and to declare that I loved her as much as God.

Her eyes rekindled and shone like chrysoprases. 'In truth?—in very truth?—as much as God!' she cried, flinging her beautiful arms around me. 'Since it is so, thou wilt come with me; thou wilt follow me whithersoever I desire. Thou wilt cast away thy ugly black habit. Thou shalt be the proudest and most envied of cavaliers; thou shalt be my lover! To be the acknowledged lover of Clarimonde, who has refused even a Pope! That will be something to feel proud of. Ah, the fair, unspeakably happy existence, the beautiful golden life we shall live together! And when shall we depart, my fair sir?'

'To-morrow! To-morrow!' I cried in my delirium.

'To-morrow, then, so let it be!' she answered. 'In the meanwhile I shall have opportunity to change my toilet, for this is a little too light and in nowise suited for a voyage. I must also forthwith notify all my friends who believe me dead, and mourn for me as deeply as they are capable of doing. The money, the dresses, the carriages—all will be ready. I shall call for thee at this same hour. Adieu, dear heart!' And she lightly touched my forehead with her lips. The lamp went out, the curtains closed again, and all became dark; a leaden, dreamless sleep fell on me and held me unconscious until the morning following.

I awoke later than usual, and the recollection of this singular adventure troubled me during the whole day. I finally persuaded myself that it was a mere vapour of my heated imagination. Nevertheless its sensations had been so vivid that it was difficult to persuade myself that they were not real, and it was not without some presentiment of what was going to happen that I got into bed at last, after having prayed God to drive far from me all thoughts of evil, and to protect the chastity of my slumber.

I soon fell into a deep sleep, and my dream was continued. The curtains again parted, and I beheld Clarimonde, not as on the former occasion, pale in her pale winding-sheet, with the violets of death upon her cheeks, but gay, sprightly, jaunty, in a superb travelling-dress of green velvet, trimmed with gold lace, and looped up on either side to allow a glimpse of satin petticoat. Her blond hair escaped in thick ringlets from beneath a broad black felt hat, decorated with white feathers whimsically twisted into various shapes. In one hand she held a little riding-whip terminated by a golden whistle. She tapped me lightly with it, and exclaimed: 'Well, my fine sleeper, is this the way you make your preparations? I thought I would find you up and dressed. Arise quickly, we have no time to lose.'

I leaped out of bed at once.

'Come, dress yourself, and let us go,' she continued, pointing to a little package she had brought with her. 'The horses are becoming impatient of delay and champing their bits at the door. We ought to have been by this time at least ten leagues distant from here.'

I dressed myself hurriedly, and she handed me the articles of apparel herself one by one, bursting into laughter from time to time at my awkwardness, as she explained to me the use of a garment when I had made a mistake. She hurriedly arranged my hair, and this done, held up before me a little pocket-mirror of Venetian crystal, rimmed with silver filigree-work, and playfully asked: 'How dost find thyself now? Wilt engage me for thy valet de chambre?'

I was no longer the same person, and I could not even recognise myself. I resembled my former self no more than a finished statue resembles a block of stone. My old face seemed but a coarse daub of the one reflected in the mirror. I was handsome, and my vanity was sensibly tickled by the metamorphosis.

> *All the doors opened before her at a touch, and we passed by the dog without awaking him.*

That elegant apparel, that richly embroidered vest had made of me a totally different personage, and I marvelled at the power of transformation owned by a few yards of cloth cut after a certain pattern. The spirit of my costume penetrated my very skin and within ten minutes more I had become something of a coxcomb.

In order to feel more at ease in my new attire, I took several turns up and down the room. Clarimonde watched me with an air of maternal pleasure, and appeared well satisfied with her work. 'Come, enough of this child's play! Let us start, Romuald, dear. We have far to go, and we may not get there in time.' She took my hand and led me forth. All the doors opened before her at a touch, and we passed by the dog without awaking him.

At the gate we found Margheritone waiting, the same swarthy groom who had once before been my escort. He held the bridles of three horses, all black like those which bore us to the castle—one for me, one for him, one for Clarimonde. Those horses must have been Spanish genets born of mares fecundated by a zephyr, for they were fleet as the wind itself, and the moon, which had just risen at our departure to light us on the way, rolled over the sky like a wheel detached from her own chariot. We beheld her on the right leaping from tree to tree, and putting herself out of breath in the effort to keep up with us. Soon we came upon a level plain where, hard by a clump of trees, a carriage with four vigorous horses awaited us. We entered it, and the postillions urged their animals into a mad gallop. I had one arm around Clarimonde's waist, and one of her hands clasped in mine; her head leaned upon my shoulder, and I felt her bosom, half bare, lightly pressing against my arm. I had never known such intense happiness. In that hour I had forgotten everything, and I no more remembered having ever been a priest than I remembered what I had been doing in my mother's womb, so great was the fascination which the evil spirit exerted upon me. From that night my nature seemed in some sort to have become halved, and there were two men within me, neither of whom knew the other. At one moment I believed myself a priest who dreamed nightly that he was a gentleman, at another that I was a gentleman who dreamed

he was a priest. I could no longer distinguish the dream from the reality, nor could I discover where the reality began or where ended the dream. The exquisite young lord and libertine railed at the priest, the priest loathed the dissolute habits of the young lord. Two spirals entangled and confounded the one with the other, yet never touching, would afford a fair representation of this bicephalic life which I lived. Despite the strange character of my condition, I do not believe that I ever inclined, even for a moment, to madness. I always retained with extreme vividness all the perceptions of my two lives. Only there was one absurd fact which I could not explain to myself—namely, that the consciousness of the same individuality existed in two men so opposite in character. It was an anomaly for which I could not account—whether I believed myself to be the curé of the little village of C———, or *Il Signor Romualdo* the titled lover of Clarimonde.

Be that as it may, I lived, at least I believed that I lived, in Venice. I have never been able to discover rightly how much of illusion and how much of reality there was in this fantastic adventure. We dwelt in a great palace on the Canaleio, filled with frescoes and statues, and containing two Titians in the noblest style of the great master, which were hung in Clarimonde's chamber. It was a palace well worthy of a king. We had each our gondola, our *barcarolli* in family livery, our music hall, and our special poet. Clarimonde always lived upon a magnificent scale; there was something of Cleopatra in her nature. As for me, I had the retinue of a prince's son, and I was regarded with as much reverential respect as though I had been of the family of one of the twelve Apostles or the four Evangelists of the Most Serene Republic. I would not have turned aside to allow even the Doge to pass, and I do not believe that since Satan fell from heaven, any creature was ever prouder or more insolent than I. I went to the Ridotto, and played with a luck which seemed absolutely infernal. I received the best of all society—the sons of ruined families, women of the theatre, shrewd knaves, parasites, hectoring swashbucklers. But notwithstanding the dissipation of such a life, I always remained faithful to Clarimonde. I loved her wildly. She would have excited satiety itself, and chained inconstancy. To have Clarimonde was to have twenty mistresses; ay, to possess all women: so mobile, so varied of aspect, so fresh in new charms was she all in herself—a very chameleon of a woman, in sooth. She made you commit with her the infidelity you would have committed with another, by donning to perfection the character, the attraction, the style of beauty of the woman who appeared to please you. She returned my love a hundred-fold, and it was in vain that the young patricians and even the Ancients of the Council of Ten made her the most magnificent proposals. A Foscari even went so far as to offer to espouse her. She rejected all his overtures. Of gold she had enough.

To have Clarimonde was to have twenty mistresses; ay, to possess all women: so mobile, so varied of aspect, so fresh in new charms was she all in herself—a very chameleon of a woman, in sooth.

She wished no longer for anything but love—a love youthful, pure, evoked by herself, and which should be a first and last passion. I would have been perfectly happy but for a cursed nightmare which recurred every night, and in which I believed myself to be a poor village curé, practising mortification and penance for my excesses during the day. Reassured by my constant association with her, I never thought further of the strange manner in which I had become acquainted with Clarimonde. But the words of the Abbé Sérapion concerning her recurred often to my memory, and never ceased to cause me uneasiness.

For some time the health of Clarimonde had not been so good as usual; her complexion grew paler day by day. The physicians who were summoned could not comprehend the nature of her malady and knew not how to treat it. They all prescribed some insignificant remedies, and never called a second time. Her paleness, nevertheless, visibly increased, and she became colder and colder, until she seemed almost as white and dead as upon that memorable night in the unknown castle. I grieved with anguish unspeakable to behold her thus slowly perishing; and she, touched by my agony, smiled upon me sweetly and sadly with the fateful smile of those who feel that they must die.

One morning I was seated at her bedside, and breakfasting from a little table placed close at hand, so that I might not be obliged to leave her for a single instant. In the act of cutting some fruit I accidentally inflicted rather a deep gash on my finger. The blood immediately gushed forth in a little purple jet, and a few drops spurted upon Clarimonde. Her eyes flashed, her face suddenly assumed an expression of savage and ferocious joy such as I had never before observed in her. She leaped out of her bed with animal agility—the agility, as it were, of an ape or a cat—and sprang upon my wound, which she commenced to suck with an air of unutterable pleasure. She swallowed the blood in little mouthfuls, slowly and carefully, like a connoisseur tasting a wine from Xeres or Syracuse. Gradually her eyelids half closed, and the pupils of her green eyes became oblong instead of round. From time to time she paused in order to kiss my hand, then she would recommence to press her lips to the lips of the wound in order to coax forth a few more ruddy drops. When she found that the blood would no longer come, she arose with eyes liquid and brilliant, rosier than a May dawn; her face full and fresh, her hand warm and moist—in fine, more beautiful than ever, and in the most perfect health.

'I shall not die! I shall not die!' she cried, clinging to my neck, half mad with joy. 'I can love thee yet for a long time. My life is thine, and all that is of me comes from thee. A few drops of thy rich and noble blood, more precious and more potent than all the elixirs of the earth, have given me back life.'

> "A few drops of thy rich and noble blood, more precious and more potent than all the elixirs of the earth, have given me back life."

This scene long haunted my memory, and inspired me with strange doubts in regard to Clarimonde; and the same evening, when slumber had transported me to my presbytery, I beheld the Abbé Sérapion, graver and more anxious of aspect than ever. He gazed attentively at me, and sorrowfully exclaimed: 'Not content with losing your soul, you now desire also to lose your body. Wretched young man, into how terrible a plight have you fallen!' The tone in which he uttered these words powerfully affected me, but in spite of its vividness even that impression was soon dissipated, and a thousand other cares erased it from my mind. At last one evening, while looking into a mirror whose traitorous position she had not taken into account, I saw Clarimonde in the act of emptying a powder into the cup of spiced wine which she had long been in the habit of preparing after our repasts. I took the cup, feigned to carry it to my lips, and then placed it on the nearest article of furniture as though intending to finish it at my leisure. Taking advantage of a moment when the fair one's back was turned, I threw the contents under the table, after which I retired to my chamber and went to bed, fully resolved not to sleep, but to watch and discover what should come of all this mystery. I did not have to wait long, Clarimonde entered in her nightdress, and having removed her apparel, crept into bed and lay down beside me. When she felt assured that I was asleep, she bared my arm, and drawing a gold pin from her hair, commenced to murmur in a low voice:

'One drop, only one drop! One ruby at the end of my needle. . . . Since thou lovest me yet, I must not die! . . . Ah, poor love! His beautiful blood, so brightly purple, I must drink it. Sleep, my only treasure! Sleep, my god, my child! I will do thee no harm; I will only take of thy life what I must to keep my own from being for ever extinguished. But that I love thee so much, I could well resolve to have other lovers whose veins I could drain; but since I have known thee all other men have become hateful to me. . . . Ah, the beautiful arm! How round it is! How white it is! How shall I ever dare to prick this pretty blue vein!' And while thus murmuring to herself she wept, and I felt her tears raining on my arm as she clasped it with her hands. At last she took the resolve, slightly punctured me with her pin, and commenced to suck up the blood which oozed from the place. Although she swallowed only a few drops, the fear of weakening me soon seized her, and she carefully tied a little band around my arm, afterward rubbing the wound with an unguent which immediately cicatrised it. Further doubts were impossible. The Abbé Sérapion was right. Notwithstanding this positive knowledge, however, I could not cease to love Clarimonde, and I would gladly of my own accord have given her all the blood she required to sustain her factitious life. Moreover, I

felt but little fear of her. The woman seemed to plead with me for the vampire, and what I had already heard and seen sufficed to reassure me completely. In those days I had plenteous veins, which would not have been so easily exhausted as at present; and I would not have thought of bargaining for my blood, drop by drop. I would rather have opened myself the veins of my arm and said to her: 'Drink, and may my love infiltrate itself throughout thy body together with my blood!' I carefully avoided ever making the least reference to the narcotic drink she had prepared for me, or to the incident of the pin, and we lived in the most perfect harmony.

Yet my priestly scruples commenced to torment me more than ever, and I was at a loss to imagine what new penance I could invent in order to mortify and subdue my flesh. Although these visions were involuntary, and though I did not actually participate in anything relating to them, I could not dare to touch the body of Christ with hands so impure and a mind defiled by such debauches whether real or imaginary. In the effort to avoid falling under the

influence of these wearisome hallucinations, I strove to prevent myself from being overcome by sleep. I held my eyelids open with my fingers, and stood for hours together leaning upright against the wall, fighting sleep with all my might; but the dust of drowsiness invariably gathered upon my eyes at last, and finding all resistance useless, I would have to let my arms fall in the extremity of despairing weariness, and the current of slumber would again bear me away to the perfidious shores. Sérapion addressed me with the most vehement exhortations, severely reproaching me for my softness and want of fervour. Finally, one day when I was more wretched than usual, he said to me: 'There is but one way by which you can obtain relief from this continual torment, and though it is an extreme measure it must be made use of; violent diseases require violent remedies. I know where Clarimonde is buried. It is necessary that we shall disinter her remains, and that you shall behold in how pitiable a state the object of your love is. Then you will no longer be tempted to lose your soul for the sake of an unclean corpse devoured by worms, and ready to crumble into dust. That will assuredly restore you to yourself.' For my part, I was so tired of this double life that I at once consented, desiring to ascertain beyond a doubt whether a priest or a gentleman had been the victim of delusion. I had become fully resolved either to kill one of the two men within me for the benefit of the other, or else to kill both, for so terrible an existence could not last long and be endured. The Abbé Sérapion provided himself with a mattock, a lever, and a lantern, and at midnight we wended our way to the cemetery of ———, the location and place of which were perfectly familiar to him. After having directed the rays of the dark lantern upon the inscriptions of several tombs, we came at last upon a great slab, half concealed by huge weeds and devoured by mosses and parasitic plants, whereupon we deciphered the opening lines of the epitaph:

Here lies Clarimonde
Who was famed in her life-time
As the fairest of women.*

* *Ici gît Clarimonde*
Qui fut de son vivant
La plus belle du monde.

The broken beauty of the lines is unavoidably lost in the translation.

'It is here without a doubt,' muttered Sérapion, and placing his lantern on the ground, he forced the point of the lever under the edge of the stone and commenced to raise it. The stone yielded, and he proceeded to work with the mattock. Darker and more silent than the night itself, I stood by and watched him do it, while he, bending over his dismal toil, streamed with sweat, panted, and his hard-coming breath seemed to have the harsh tone of a death rattle. It was a weird scene, and had any persons from without beheld us, they would assuredly have taken us rather for profane wretches and shroud-stealers than for priests of God. There was something grim and fierce in Sérapion's zeal which lent him the air of a demon rather than of an apostle or an angel, and his great aquiline face, with all its stern features, brought out in strong relief by the lantern-light, had something fearsome in it which enhanced the unpleasant fancy. I felt an icy sweat come out upon my forehead in huge beads, and my hair stood up with a hideous fear. Within the depths of my own heart I felt that the act of the austere Sérapion was an abominable sacrilege; and I could have prayed that a triangle of fire would issue from the entrails of the dark clouds, heavily rolling above us, to reduce him to cinders. The owls which had been nestling in the cypress-trees, startled by the gleam of the lantern, flew against it from time to time, striking their dusty wings against its panes, and uttering plaintive cries of lamentation; wild foxes yelped in the far darkness, and a thousand sinister noises detached themselves from the silence. At last Sérapion's mattock struck the coffin itself, making its planks re-echo with a deep sonorous sound, with that terrible sound nothingness utters when

stricken. He wrenched apart and tore up the lid, and I beheld Clarimonde, pallid as a figure of marble, with hands joined; her white winding-sheet made but one fold from her head to her feet. A little crimson drop sparkled like a speck of dew at one corner of her colourless mouth. Sérapion, at this spectacle, burst into fury: 'Ah, thou art here, demon! Impure courtesan! Drinker of blood and gold!' And he flung holy water upon the corpse and the coffin, over which he traced the sign of the cross with his sprinkler. Poor Clarimonde had no sooner been touched by the blessed spray than her beautiful body crumbled into dust, and became only a shapeless and frightful mass of cinders and half-calcined bones.

BOUNCE BACK

The old legend that vampires must sleep in coffins most likely arose from reports from gravediggers who saw corpses suddenly sit up in their coffins. This unusual occurrence can now be chalked up to the decomposition process.

'Behold your mistress, my Lord Romuald!' cried the inexorable priest, as he pointed to these sad remains. 'Will you be easily tempted after this to promenade on the Lido or at Fusina with your beauty?' I covered my face with my hands, a vast ruin had taken place within me. I returned to my presbytery, and the noble Lord Romuald, the lover of Clarimonde, separated himself from the poor priest with whom he had kept such strange company so long. But once only, the following night, I saw Clarimonde. She said to me, as she had said the first time at the portals of the church: 'Unhappy man! Unhappy man! What hast thou done? Wherefore have hearkened to that imbecile priest? Wert thou not happy? And what harm had I ever done thee that thou shouldst violate my poor tomb, and lay bare the miseries of my nothingness? All communication between our souls and our bodies is henceforth for ever broken. Adieu! Thou wilt yet regret me!' She vanished in air as smoke, and I never saw her more.

Alas! she spoke truly indeed. I have regretted her more than once, and I regret her still. My soul's peace has been very dearly bought. The love of God was not too much to replace such a love as hers. And this, brother, is the story of my youth. Never gaze upon a woman, and walk abroad only with eyes ever fixed upon the ground; for however chaste and watchful one may be, the error of a single moment is enough to make one lose eternity.

Not all vampires cringe in the bright light of the sun. In Anne Rice's *Interview with a Vampire*, the ancients, such as Lord Ruthven and Varney, are capable of walking in the sunlight without dying. And the vampires of Stephenie Meyer's popular *Twilight* series break from tradition in many ways by walking in the sunlight and being immune to holy items. The rare disease porphyria causes many vampire-like symptoms, such as sensitivity to sunlight, hairiness, and reddish-brown teeth. In some cases, the patient eventually goes mad.

13

FROM THE CABINET
OF DR. POLIDORI

So we'll go no more a-roving
So late into the night,
Though the heart be still as loving,
And the moon be still as bright.

—LORD BYRON

Horror devotees will recall the story of the infamous gathering at a lake house outside of Geneva, Switzerland, in the summer of 1816, where a small party celebrated the settling darkness by reading ghost stories aloud to one another. Present were the host, Lord Byron, and his guests: Percy Bysshe Shelley, Mary Wollstonecraft (Shelley) and her sister, and Lord Byron's physician—John William Polidori. At the prompting of Byron, pens were set to paper to write ghost stories of their own. Here the groundwork was laid for what would become Mary Shelley's *Frankenstein, or the Modern Prometheus*. Percy Bysshe Shelley himself wrote *Fragments of a Ghost Story*, and Byron wrote something called *Fragment of a Novel*. This "fragment" became the basis for Polidori's *The Vampyre, A Tale*—the first vampire novel published in English, some seventy years before Bram Stoker's *Dracula*.

Polidori, who was also a writer and poet in his own right, traveled with Byron throughout Europe. One cannot help but imagine the stormy evenings and candlelit dinner conversations that inspired the tales of terror and vampiric imaginings that manifested into Polidori's work. Admittedly, his writing is nowhere near on par with Mary Shelley or Byron, but nonetheless, it is a valuable contribution to horror literature. Of particular value is the cultural and folkloric introduction that precedes the heart of the novel, describing vampires from around the world. Following is a brief excerpt from Polidori's introduction.

INTRODUCTION TO *The Vampyre, A Tale*
[AN EXCERPT]
by *John William Polidori*

The superstition upon which this tale is founded is very general in the East. Among the Arabians it appears to be common: it did not, however, extend itself to the Greeks until after the establishment of Christianity; and it has only assumed its present form since the division of the Latin and Greek churches; at which time, the idea becoming prevalent, that a Latin body could not corrupt if buried in their territory, it gradually increased, and formed the subject of many wonderful stories, still extant, of the dead rising from their graves, and feeding upon the blood of the young and beautiful. In the West it spread, with some slight variation, all over Hungary, Poland, Austria, and Lorraine, where the belief existed, that vampyres nightly imbibed a certain portion of the blood of their victims, who became emaciated, lost their strength, and speedily died of consumptions; whilst these human blood-suckers fattened—and their veins became distended to such a state of repletion, as to cause the blood to flow from all the passages of their bodies, and even from the very pores of their skins.

In the London Journal, of March, 1732, is a curious, and, of course, credible account of a particular case of vampyrism, which is stated to have occurred at Madreyga, in Hungary. It appears, that upon an examination of the commander-in-chief and magistrates of the place, they positively and

unanimously affirmed, that, about five years before, a certain Heyduke, named Arnold Paul, had been heard to say, that, at Cassovia, on the frontiers of the Turkish Servia, he had been tormented by a vampyre, but had found a way to rid himself of the evil, by eating some of the earth out of the vampyre's grave, and rubbing himself with his blood. This precaution, however, did not prevent him from becoming a vampyre himself; for, about twenty or thirty days after his death and burial, many persons complained of having been tormented by him, and a deposition was made, that four persons had been deprived of life by his attacks. To prevent further mischief, the inhabitants having consulted their Hadagni, took up the body, and found it (as is supposed to be usual in cases of vampyrism) fresh, and entirely free from corruption, and emitting at the mouth, nose, and ears, pure and florid blood. Proof having been thus obtained, they resorted to the accustomed remedy. A stake was driven entirely through the heart and body of Arnold Paul, at which he is reported to have cried out as dreadfully as if he had been alive. This done, they cut off his head, burned his body, and threw the ashes into his grave. The same measures were adopted with the corpses of those persons who had previously died from vampyrism, lest they should, in their turn, become agents upon others who survived them.

NOW WHY WOULD YOU
WANT TO DO THAT?

If you decide you don't want to be beautiful, everlasting, and awesome after all, here are a few anti-vampire measures:

- Drink vampire ashes if you think you've been bitten by a vampire.

- Eat bread soaked in vampire blood to keep them away.

- Vampires can't cross a threshold unless invited. (But remember, they can read your thoughts!)

No word on how to prepare vampire ashes or how to get their blood. Perhaps if you ask nicely . . .

14

DEAD NEWS
TRAVELS FAST

The best argument I know for an immortal life is the existence of a man who deserves one.

—WILLIAM JAMES

This wonderful short story, "Dracula's Guest," was one of several shorter works published in 1914 by Bram Stoker's widow, Florence, after his death. In her preface to the original collection she writes:

> A few months before the lamented death of my husband—I might say even as the shadow of death was over him—he planned three series of short stories for publication, and the present volume is one of them. To his original list of stories in this book, I have added an hitherto unpublished episode from *Dracula*. It was originally excised owing to the length of the book, and

may prove of interest to the many readers of what is considered my husband's most remarkable work. The other stories have already been published in English and American periodicals. Had my husband lived longer, he might have seen fit to revise this work, which is mainly from the earlier years of his strenuous life. But, as fate has entrusted to me the issuing of it, I consider it fitting and proper to let it go forth practically as it was left by him.

Florence Bram Stoker

Her love for him and his works comes across in this preface. And though Stoker thought this work not ready for publication, it is a nearly perfect story. In just a few pages, readers are transported to icy Munich, on a carriage ride outside the city on none other than Walpurgis Nacht—the night of the witches! Wolves howl, a storm thunders in, and a city of the dead becomes the only shelter for our hero.

And I ask you, who wouldn't want to be invited to the castle as Dracula's esteemed guest?

DRACULA'S GUEST

by Bram Stoker

When we started for our drive the sun was shining brightly on Munich, and the air was full of the joyousness of early summer. Just as we were about to depart, Herr Delbrück (the maître d'hôtel of the Quatre Saisons, where I was staying) came down, bareheaded, to the carriage and, after wishing me a pleasant drive, said to the coachman, still holding his hand on the handle of the carriage door:

'Remember you are back by nightfall. The sky looks bright but there is a shiver in the north wind that says there may be a sudden storm. But I am sure you will not be late.' Here he smiled, and added, 'for you know what night it is.'

Johann answered with an emphatic, 'Ja, mein Herr,' and, touching his hat, drove off quickly. When we had cleared the town, I said, after signalling to him to stop:

'Tell me, Johann, what is tonight?'

He crossed himself, as he answered laconically: 'Walpurgis nacht.' Then he took out his watch, a great, old-fashioned German silver thing as big as a turnip, and looked at it, with his eyebrows gathered together and a little impatient shrug of his shoulders. I realised that this was his way of respectfully protesting against the unnecessary delay, and sank back in the carriage, merely motioning him to proceed. He started off rapidly, as if to make up for lost time. Every now and then the horses seemed to throw up their heads and sniffed the air suspiciously. On such occasions I often looked round in alarm. The road was pretty bleak, for we were traversing a sort of high, wind-swept plateau. As we drove, I saw a road that looked but little used, and which seemed to dip through a little, winding valley. It looked so inviting that, even at the risk of offending him, I called Johann to stop—and when he had pulled up, I told him I would like to drive down that road. He made all sorts of excuses, and frequently crossed himself as he spoke. This somewhat piqued my curiosity, so I asked him various questions. He answered fencingly, and repeatedly looked at his watch in protest. Finally I said:

'Well, Johann, I want to go down this road. I shall not ask you to come unless you like; but tell me why you do not like to go, that is all I ask.' For answer he seemed to throw himself off the box, so quickly did he reach the ground. Then he stretched out his hands appealingly to me, and implored me not to go. There was just enough of English mixed with the German for me to understand the drift of his talk. He seemed always just about to tell me something—the very idea of which evidently frightened him; but each time he pulled himself up, saying, as he crossed himself: 'Walpurgis nacht!'

I tried to argue with him, but it was difficult to argue with a man when I did not know his language. The advantage certainly rested with him, for although he began to speak in English, of a very crude and broken kind, he always got excited and broke into his native tongue—and every time he did so, he looked at his watch. Then the horses became restless and sniffed the air. At this he grew very pale, and, looking around in a frightened way, he suddenly jumped forward, took them by the bridles and led them on some twenty feet. I followed, and asked why he had done this. For answer he crossed himself, pointed to the spot we had left and drew his carriage in the direction of the other road, indicating a cross, and said, first in German, then in English: 'Buried him—him what killed themselves.'

I remembered the old custom of burying suicides at cross-roads: 'Ah! I see, a suicide. How interesting!' But for the life of me I could not make out why the horses were frightened.

Whilst we were talking, we heard a sort of sound between a yelp and a bark. It was far away; but the horses got very restless, and it took Johann all his time to quiet them. He was pale, and said, 'It sounds like a wolf—but yet there are no wolves here now.'

'No?' I said, questioning him; 'isn't it long since the wolves were so near the city?'

'Long, long,' he answered, 'in the spring and summer; but with the snow the wolves have been here not so long.'

Whilst he was petting the horses and trying to quiet them, dark clouds drifted rapidly across the sky. The sunshine passed away, and a breath of cold wind seemed to drift past us. It was only a breath, however, and more in the nature of a warning than a fact, for the sun came out brightly again. Johann looked under his lifted hand at the horizon and said:

'The storm of snow, he comes before long time.' Then he looked at his watch again, and, straightway holding his reins firmly—for the horses were still pawing the ground restlessly and shaking their heads—he climbed to his box as though the time had come for proceeding on our journey.

I felt a little obstinate and did not at once get into the carriage.

'Tell me,' I said, 'about this place where the road leads,' and I pointed down.

Again he crossed himself and mumbled a prayer, before he answered, 'It is unholy.'

'What is unholy?' I enquired.

'The village.'

'Then there is a village?'

'No, no. No one lives there hundreds of years.' My curiosity was piqued, 'But you said there was a village.'

'There was.'

'Where is it now?'

Whereupon he burst out into a long story in German and English, so mixed up that I could not quite understand exactly what he said, but roughly I gathered that long ago, hundreds of years, men had died there and been buried in their graves; and sounds were heard under the clay, and when the graves were opened, men

Men had died there and been buried in their graves; and sounds were heard under the clay, and when the graves were opened, men and women were found rosy with life, and their mouths red with blood.

and women were found rosy with life, and their mouths red with blood. And so, in haste to save their lives (aye, and their souls!—and here he crossed himself) those who were left fled away to other places, where the living lived, and the dead were dead and not—not something. He was evidently afraid to speak the last words. As he proceeded with his narration, he grew more and more excited. It seemed as if his imagination had got hold of him, and he ended in a perfect paroxysm of fear—white-faced, perspiring, trembling and looking round him, as if expecting that some dreadful presence would manifest itself there in the bright sunshine on the open plain. Finally, in an agony of desperation, he cried:

'Walpurgis nacht!' and pointed to the carriage for me to get in. All my English blood rose at this, and, standing back, I said:

'You are afraid, Johann—you are afraid. Go home; I shall return alone; the walk will do me good.' The carriage door was open. I took from the seat my oak walking-stick—which I always carry on my holiday excursions—and closed the door, pointing back to Munich, and said, 'Go home, Johann—Walpurgis nacht doesn't concern Englishmen.'

Since its first publication in 1897, Bram Stoker's *Dracula* has never gone out of print. Scholars like to point to Christian allegory as his inspiration, while others say the story reflects the psycho-sexual anxieties of the Victorian era.

The horses were now more restive than ever, and Johann was trying to hold them in, while excitedly imploring me not to do anything so foolish. I pitied the poor fellow, he was deeply in earnest; but all the same I could not help laughing. His English was quite gone now. In his anxiety he had forgotten that his only means of making me understand was to talk my language, so he jabbered away in his native German. It began to be a little tedious. After giving the direction, 'Home!' I turned to go down the cross-road into the valley.

With a despairing gesture, Johann turned his horses towards Munich. I leaned on my stick and looked after him. He went slowly along the road for a while: then there came over the crest of the hill a man tall and thin. I could see so much in the distance. When he drew near the horses, they began to jump and kick about, then to scream with terror. Johann could not hold them in; they bolted down the road, running away madly. I watched them out of sight, then looked for the stranger, but I found that he, too, was gone.

With a light heart I turned down the side road through the deepening valley to which Johann had objected. There was not the slightest reason, that I could see, for his objection; and I daresay I tramped for a couple of hours without thinking of time or distance, and certainly without seeing a person or a house. So far as the place was concerned, it was desolation, itself. But I did not notice this particularly till, on turning a bend in the road, I came upon a scattered fringe of wood; then I recognised that I had been impressed unconsciously by the desolation of the region through which I had passed.

I sat down to rest myself, and began to look around. It struck me that it was considerably colder than it had been at the commencement of my walk—a sort of sighing sound seemed to be around me, with, now and then, high overhead, a sort of muffled roar. Looking upwards I noticed that great thick clouds were drifting rapidly across the sky from North to South at a great height. There were signs of coming storm in some lofty stratum of the air. I was a little chilly, and, thinking that it was the sitting still after the exercise of walking, I resumed my journey.

 The ground I passed over was now much more picturesque. There were no striking objects that the eye might single out; but in all there was a charm of beauty. I took little heed of time and it was only when the deepening twilight forced itself upon me that I began to think of how I should find my way home. The brightness of the day had gone. The air was cold, and the drifting of clouds high overhead was more marked. They were accompanied by a sort of far-away rushing sound, through which seemed to come at intervals that mysterious cry which the driver had said came from a wolf. For a while I hesitated. I had said I would see the deserted village, so on I went, and presently came on a wide stretch of open country, shut in by hills all

around. Their sides were covered with trees which spread down to the plain, dotting, in clumps, the gentler slopes and hollows which showed here and there. I followed with my eye the winding of the road, and saw that it curved close to one of the densest of these clumps and was lost behind it.

As I looked there came a cold shiver in the air, and the snow began to fall. I thought of the miles and miles of bleak country I had passed, and then hurried on to seek the shelter of the wood in front. Darker and darker grew the sky, and faster and heavier fell the snow, till the earth before and around me was a glistening white carpet the further edge of which was lost in misty vagueness. The road was here but crude, and when on the level its boundaries were not so marked, as when it passed through the cuttings; and in a little while I found that I must have strayed from it, for I missed underfoot the hard surface, and my feet sank deeper in the grass and moss. Then the wind grew stronger and blew with ever increasing force, till I was fain to run before it. The air became icy-cold, and in spite of my exercise I began to suffer. The snow was now falling so thickly and whirling around me in such rapid eddies that I could hardly keep my eyes open. Every now and then the heavens were torn asunder by vivid lightning, and in the flashes I could see ahead of me a great mass of trees, chiefly yew and cypress all heavily coated with snow.

I was soon amongst the shelter of the trees, and there, in comparative silence, I could hear the rush of the wind high overhead. Presently the blackness of the storm had become merged in the darkness of the night. By-and-by the storm seemed to be passing away: it now only came in fierce puffs or blasts. At such moments the weird sound of the wolf appeared to be echoed by many similar sounds around me.

Now and again, through the black mass of drifting cloud, came a straggling ray of moonlight, which lit up the expanse, and showed me that I was at the edge of a dense mass of cypress and yew trees. As the snow had ceased to fall, I walked out from the shelter and began to investigate more closely. It appeared to me that, amongst so many old foundations as I had passed, there might be still standing a house in which, though in ruins, I could find some sort of shelter for a while. As I skirted the edge of the copse, I found that a low wall encircled it, and following this I presently found an opening. Here the cypresses formed an alley leading up to a square mass of some kind of building. Just as I caught sight of this, however, the drifting clouds obscured the moon, and I passed up the path in darkness. The wind must have grown

colder, for I felt myself shiver as I walked; but there was hope of shelter, and I groped my way blindly on.

I stopped, for there was a sudden stillness. The storm had passed; and, perhaps in sympathy with nature's silence, my heart seemed to cease to beat. But this was only momentarily; for suddenly the moonlight broke through the clouds, showing me that I was in a graveyard, and that the square object before me was a great massive tomb of marble, as white as the snow that lay on and all around it. With the moonlight there came a fierce sigh of the storm, which appeared to resume its course with a long, low howl, as of many dogs or wolves. I was awed and shocked, and felt the cold perceptibly grow upon me till it seemed to grip me by the heart. Then while the flood of moonlight still fell on the marble tomb, the storm gave further evidence of renewing, as though it was returning on its track. Impelled by some sort of fascination, I approached the sepulchre to see what it was, and why such a thing stood alone in such a place. I walked around it, and read, over the Doric door, in German:

COUNTESS DOLINGEN OF GRATZ IN
STYRIA SOUGHT AND FOUND DEATH 1801

On the top of the tomb, seemingly driven through the solid marble—for the structure was composed of a few vast blocks of stone—was a great iron spike or stake. On going to the back I saw, graven in great Russian letters:

'The dead travel fast.'

There was something so weird and uncanny about the whole thing that it gave me a turn and made me feel quite faint. I began to wish, for the first time, that I had taken Johann's advice. Here a thought struck me, which came under almost mysterious circumstances and with a terrible shock. This was Walpurgis Night!

Walpurgis Night, when, according to the belief of millions of people, the devil was abroad—when the graves were opened and the dead came forth and walked. When all evil things of earth and air and water held revel. This very place the driver had specially shunned. This was the depopulated village of centuries ago. This was where the suicide lay; and this was the place where I was alone—unmanned, shivering with cold in a shroud of snow with a wild storm gathering again upon me! It took all my philosophy, all the religion I had been taught, all my courage, not to collapse in a paroxysm of fright.

And now a perfect tornado burst upon me. The ground shook as though thousands of horses thundered across it; and this time the storm bore on its icy wings, not snow, but great hailstones which drove with such violence that they might have come from the thongs of Balearic slingers—hailstones that beat down leaf and branch and made

Walpurgis Night, when, according to the belief of millions of people, the devil was abroad—when the graves were opened and the dead came forth and walked. When all evil things of earth and air and water held revel.

the shelter of the cypresses of no more avail than though their stems were standing-corn. At the first I had rushed to the nearest tree; but I was soon fain to leave it and seek the only spot that seemed to afford refuge, the deep Doric doorway of the marble tomb. There, crouching against the massive bronze door, I gained a certain amount of protection from the beating of the hailstones, for now they only drove against me as they ricocheted from the ground and the side of the marble.

As I leaned against the door, it moved slightly and opened inwards. The shelter of even a tomb was welcome in that pitiless tempest, and I was about to enter it when there came a flash of forked-lightning that lit up the whole expanse of the heavens. In the instant, as I am a living man, I saw, as my eyes were turned into the darkness of the tomb, a beautiful woman, with rounded cheeks and red lips, seemingly sleeping on a bier. As the thunder broke overhead, I was grasped as by the hand of a giant and hurled out into the

storm. The whole thing was so sudden that, before I could realise the shock, moral as well as physical, I found the hailstones beating me down. At the same time I had a strange, dominating feeling that I was not alone. I looked towards the tomb. Just then there came another blinding flash, which seemed to strike the iron stake that surmounted the tomb and to pour through to the earth, blasting and crumbling the marble, as in a burst of flame. The dead woman rose for a moment of agony, while she was lapped in the flame, and her bitter scream of pain was drowned in the thundercrash. The last thing I heard was this mingling of dreadful sound, as again I was seized in the giant-grasp and dragged away, while the hailstones beat on me, and the air around seemed reverberant with the howling of wolves. The last sight that I remembered was a vague, white, moving mass, as if all the graves around me had sent out the phantoms of their sheeted-dead, and that they were closing in on me through the white cloudiness of the driving hail.

Gradually there came a sort of vague beginning of consciousness; then a sense of weariness that was dreadful. For a time I remembered nothing; but slowly my senses returned. My feet seemed positively racked with pain, yet I could not move them. They seemed to be numbed. There was an icy feeling at the back of my neck and all down my spine, and my ears, like my feet, were dead, yet in torment; but there was in my breast a sense of warmth which was, by comparison, delicious. It was as a nightmare—a physical nightmare, if one may use such an expression; for some heavy weight on my chest made it difficult for me to breathe.

This period of semi-lethargy seemed to remain a long time, and as it faded away I must have slept or swooned. Then came a sort of loathing, like the first stage of sea-sickness, and a wild desire to be free from something— I knew not what. A vast stillness enveloped me, as though all the world were asleep or dead—only broken by the low panting as of some animal close to me. I felt a warm rasping at my throat, then came a consciousness of the awful truth, which chilled me to the heart and sent the blood surging up through my brain. Some great animal was lying on me and now licking my throat. I feared to stir, for some instinct of prudence bade me lie still; but the brute seemed to realise that there was now some change in me, for it raised its head. Through my eyelashes I saw above me the two great flaming eyes of a gigantic wolf. Its sharp white teeth gleamed in the gaping red mouth, and I could feel its hot breath fierce and acrid upon me.

For another spell of time I remembered no more. Then I became conscious of a low growl, followed by a yelp, renewed again and again. Then, seemingly very far away, I heard a 'Holloa! holloa!' as of many voices calling in unison. Cautiously I raised my head and looked in the direction whence the sound came; but the cemetery blocked my view. The wolf still continued to yelp in a strange way, and a red glare began to move round the grove of cypresses, as though following the sound. As the voices drew closer, the wolf yelped faster and louder. I feared to make either sound or motion. Nearer came the red glow, over the white pall which stretched into the darkness around me. Then all at once from beyond the trees there came at a trot a troop of horsemen bearing torches. The wolf rose from my breast and made for the cemetery. I saw one of the horsemen (soldiers by their caps and their long military cloaks) raise his carbine and take aim. A companion knocked up his arm, and I heard the ball whizz over my head. He had evidently taken my body for that of the wolf. Another sighted the animal as it slunk away, and a shot followed. Then, at a gallop, the troop rode forward—some towards me, others following the wolf as it disappeared amongst the snow-clad cypresses.

As they drew nearer I tried to move, but was powerless, although I could see and hear all that went on around me. Two or three of the soldiers jumped from their horses and knelt beside me. One of them raised my head, and placed his hand over my heart.

'Good news, comrades!' he cried. 'His heart still beats!'

Then some brandy was poured down my throat; it put vigour into me, and I was able to open my eyes fully and look around. Lights and shadows were moving among the trees, and I heard men call to one another. They drew together, uttering frightened exclamations; and the lights flashed as the others came pouring out of the cemetery pell-mell, like men possessed. When the further ones came close to us, those who were around me asked them eagerly:

'Well, have you found him?'

The reply rang out hurriedly:

'No! no! Come away quick—quick! This is no place to stay, and on this of all nights!'

'What was it?' was the question, asked in all manner of keys. The answer came variously and all indefinitely as though the men were moved by some common impulse to speak, yet were restrained by some common fear from giving their thoughts.

'It—it—indeed!' gibbered one, whose wits had plainly given out for the moment.

'A wolf—and yet not a wolf!' another put in shudderingly.

'No use trying for him without the sacred bullet,' a third remarked in a more ordinary manner.

'Serve us right for coming out on this night! Truly we have earned our thousand marks!' were the ejaculations of a fourth.

'There was blood on the broken marble,' another said after a pause—'the lightning never brought that there. And for him—is he safe? Look at his throat! See, comrades, the wolf has been lying on him and keeping his blood warm.'

The officer looked at my throat and replied:

'He is all right; the skin is not pierced. What does it all mean? We should never have found him but for the yelping of the wolf.'

'What became of it?' asked the man who was holding up my head, and who seemed the least panic-stricken of the party, for his hands were steady and without tremor. On his sleeve was the chevron of a petty officer.

'It went to its home,' answered the man, whose long face was pallid, and who actually shook with terror as he glanced around him fearfully. 'There are graves enough there in which it may lie. Come, comrades—come quickly! Let us leave this cursed spot.'

The officer raised me to a sitting posture, as he uttered a word of command; then several men placed me upon a horse. He sprang to the saddle behind me, took me in his arms, gave the word to advance; and, turning our faces away from the cypresses, we rode away in swift, military order.

As yet my tongue refused its office, and I was perforce silent. I must have fallen asleep; for the next thing I remembered was finding myself standing up, supported by a soldier on each side of me. It was almost broad daylight, and to the north a red streak of sunlight was reflected, like a path of blood, over the waste of snow. The officer was telling the men to say nothing of what they had seen, except that they found an English stranger, guarded by a large dog.

'Dog! that was no dog,' cut in the man who had exhibited such fear. 'I think I know a wolf when I see one.'

The young officer answered calmly: 'I said a dog.'

'Dog!' reiterated the other ironically. It was evident that his courage was rising with the sun; and, pointing to me, he said, 'Look at his throat. Is that the work of a dog, master?'

Instinctively I raised my hand to my throat, and as I touched it I cried out in pain. The men crowded round to look, some stooping down from their saddles; and again there came the calm voice of the young officer:

'A dog, as I said. If aught else were said we should only be laughed at.'

I was then mounted behind a trooper, and we rode on into the suburbs of Munich. Here we came across a stray carriage, into which I was lifted, and it was driven off to the Quatre Saisons—the young officer accompanying me, whilst a trooper followed with his horse, and the others rode off to their barracks.

When we arrived, Herr Delbrück rushed so quickly down the steps to meet me, that it was apparent he had been watching within. Taking me by both hands he solicitously led me in. The officer saluted me and was turning to withdraw, when I recognised his purpose, and insisted that he should come to my rooms. Over a glass of wine I warmly thanked him and his brave comrades for saving me. He replied simply that he was more than glad, and that Herr Delbrück had at the first taken steps to make all the searching party pleased; at which ambiguous utterance the maître d'hôtel smiled, while the officer pleaded duty and withdrew.

'But Herr Delbrück,' I enquired, 'how and why was it that the soldiers searched for me?'

He shrugged his shoulders, as if in depreciation of his own deed, as he replied:

'I was so fortunate as to obtain leave from the commander of the regiment in which I served, to ask for volunteers.'

'But how did you know I was lost?' I asked.

'The driver came hither with the remains of his carriage, which had been upset when the horses ran away.'

'But surely you would not send a search-party of soldiers merely on this account?'

'Oh, no!' he answered; 'but even before the coachman arrived, I had this telegram from the Boyar whose guest you are,' and he took from his pocket a telegram which he handed to me, and I read:

Bistritz.

Be careful of my guest–his safety is most precious to me. Should aught happen to him, or if he be missed, spare nothing to find him and ensure his safety. He is English and therefore adventurous. There are often dangers from snow and wolves and night. Lose not a moment if you suspect harm to him. I answer your zeal with my fortune.

—Dracula.

As I held the telegram in my hand, the room seemed to whirl around me; and, if the attentive maître d'hôtel had not caught me, I think I should have fallen. There was something so strange in all this, something so weird and impossible to imagine, that there grew on me a sense of my being in some way the sport of opposite forces—the mere vague idea of which seemed in a way to paralyse me. I was certainly under some form of mysterious protection. From a distant country had come, in the very nick of time, a message that took me out of the danger of the snow-sleep and the jaws of the wolf.

> The man who encompasses heaven and hell is a perfect man. But there are many heavens and more hells.
>
> —George Vireck, from *The House of the Vampire*, the first psychic vampire novel.

15

VAMPIRES OLD
AND NEW

The word *vampire* made its appearance in the common lexicon circa 1734, but in earlier literature it appears with the spelling *vampyre*. Many scholars believe the word comes from the Hungarian *vampir* or Turkish *upyr*, meaning "witch." Today's vampire isn't just the coffin-sleeping, tuxedo-wearing, pale-skinned vamp of yore. In fact, as Father Sebastiaan, renowned fangsmith, author, and prominent member of the Living Vampire community puts it, "Vampires have evolved, morphed, and transformed from ancient blood sucking revenants to your loving and friendly neighbors, family, friends, and even your cable man."

I can say without a dark shadow of doubt that I'd be thrilled to have a vampire handyman (I do keep my curtains drawn to block out the light most of the time, after all). Here are a few stories of modern vampires, ancient vampires, and some immortals in between.

Real Vampires of Atlanta

Nearly every vampire alive today was born to human parents.

—J.M. Dixon

Vampires and witches share a common history of persecution for supposedly supernatural powers, including the ability to cause plagues and curses to livestock and humans. In an interview with members of the Global Vampire Community, Merticus, a member of the Atlanta Vampire Alliance, defends the vampire against common misconceptions that living vampires are evil or cruel or psychopathic:

> Real vampires are too often mistakenly thrust into the same category of ritual animal or human sacrifice, fetishism or classified as some other form of paraphilia, fanatical religious expression or cults, and labeled as unstable threats to themselves and others. We are almost universally not the individuals who commit ritualistic crimes involving human sacrifice, cannibalism, and murder as sometimes portrayed by the media. We resent when the actions of mentally disturbed individuals are lauded as an example of an inextricable link to modern vampirism; some going further to insinuate that our subculture encourages and condones such behavior. Those who commit acts of violence or similarly egregious behavior within the vampire community are

almost universally roleplayers or dabblers who've lost touch with reality or long-term psychologically imbalanced persons who pose a threat to society whether they label themselves as a "vampire" or not.

Vampire Holidays

According to Father Sebastiaan, author of *Vampyre Sanguinomicon* and *Vampyre Magick*, the Living Vampires, or Strigoi VII, celebrate six major holidays:

- The Masque from October 30th to November 1st. Known as the Celebration of the Twilight Festival, this is the equivalent of the Vampire New Year and is most traditionally celebrated with a masquerade ball.

- The Nightside Mass during Yule or Winter Solstice—on or around December 21st in the Northern Hemisphere, in the Southern Hemisphere it is celebrated on or around June 20th. Known as Their Long Night, this is the night when a grand astral convergence takes place when, at the stroke of midnight, all Vampyres converge.

- The Crimson Mass or Anti-Valentine's Day on February 14th. A celebration of the existence of eternal love—an excellent night for harvesting the energy of lovers.

- Night of Fire from April 30th to May 1st. Held on the night traditionally known in Germany as Walpurgisnacht or Witches' Night, today's Living Vampire knows this night as A Celebration of the Dragon Festival. Bonfires are lit and, symbolically, it is a time of purification and rebirth.

- The Long Day Mass during Summer Solstice, June 21st. A celebration marking the importance of a vampire's dayside life, of the mundane and the five senses.

- The Wild Hunt in August. A movable feast known as Celebration of the Bast Festival, it is tied in with the ending of summer and the harvest, and it commemorates the primal vampire nature. It is one of the wildest nights of the year.

Vampires in legend are known to shape-change into a bat, wolf, or mist, but in reality this is virtually impossible to achieve with the corporeal layer of reality and can only be done in the ethereal and astral realms.

—Father Sebastiaan, from *Vampyre Magick*

Takes a Lot of Heart

In the winter of 1892, a nineteen-year-old girl from Rhode Island named Mercy Brown died unexpectedly from an unknown illness. Soon after her death, people from her community started seeing her walking around town. They dug up her body in the spring to find it looked very much alive. They promptly removed her heart to prevent her from wandering.

BEAUTY IS IN THE EYE OF THE BEHOLDER

In 2010, a new trend started called the vampire face-lift. The idea is to take blood from other parts of your body and inject it into your face. Dr. Anthony Youn told *Salon.com*, "Alas, it won't make your face immortal or make your skin paler or anything like that."

One of the most prolific murderers of all time was one Elizabeth Bathory, who lived in the 1600s in Transylvania. She is reputed to have killed more than 600 women and girls to drink and bathe in their blood, which she believed would keep her young. The niece of the king of Poland, she was not killed when the murders were discovered, but instead was walled up in her castle until her death.

STOP ME IF YOU'VE HEARD THIS ONE

During the fifteenth century, the Romanian prince, Vlad III, killed his enemies by impaling them with wooden stakes through the heart or stomach. After one bloody battle, the countryside was covered with rotting staked corpses and came to be known as the Forest of the Impaled. He then became known as Vlad the Impaler. Interestingly, Vlad's father had been in the Order of the Dragon for many years and was often called Vlad Dracul. Therefore, in the Order of the Dragon tradition, Vlad Junior was also known as Dracula, son of the dragon. (From *Dark Banquet* by Bill Schutt.)

FANCY FEAST

In London in 1839, Highgate Cemetery was specifically reserved for the elite. These days, the cemetery is home to a petrifying vampire. Years of neglect led to the abandonment of Highgate Cemetery but reported sightings of a large figure with red eyes started in the late 1960s. One evening in 1971, a young girl was walking past the cemetery when a very pale, very tall man cloaked in black shoved her to the ground with such force, she sustained bruises all over her body. Fortunately, a car pulled up to the scene just in time and the man disappeared instantly.

CORPSE TO CORPSE

Chinese vampires were originally called corpse hoppers and had blood-red eyes and long claws. Their strong sexual desires led them to attack women. Some had the ability to fly or change into wolves.

THE TRANSYLVANIAN TABLETS

In 1961, archaeologists digging into a prehistoric mound in the Transylvanian village of Tartaria made a startling discovery—several small clay tablets with bizarre inscriptions on them. Some believed the inscriptions to be sigils or magical signs, and others believed that they were important documents left behind for the singular purpose of being found— time capsules, perhaps. Using the modern method of carbon dating, the objects' origin was placed at around 4000 BC. The writing was believed to be of Mesopotamian origin, specifically Sumerian, the first written language. Could this discovery mean the origins of writing began in the wild backwoods of Transylvania? The three tablets were found in the lowest layer of the dig. They were in a sacrificial pit within a burial mound, and the pit also contained some scattered human bones. The bones bore symbols quite similar to the inscriptions on the tablets; the symbols were both from Sumer and from the highly advanced Minoan civilizations of Crete. But if the carbon dating is accurate, the tablets were made by a primitive Stone Age agricultural tribe known as the Vinca. The Vinca predated Sumerian writing by one millennium and the Minoan writing by two thousand years. Most scholars believe that the inscriptions were magical ciphers—spells and secret codes of this ancient farming tribe. The hash marks, swirls, *x*'s, and shapes on the three tablets cast a spell over mystery lovers too. (From *The Book of the Bizarre* by Varla Ventura.)

BLOOD THIRSTY GODDESSES

The ancient Indian goddess Kali had powerful cravings for human blood. The Egyptian goddess Sekhmet was also known to be a blood drinker.

FEMME FATALE

In 2006, archaeologists found the remains of a female vampire in Italy. Forensic archaeologist Matteo Borrini discovered the remains and noticed a brick forced into her jaw. He reported his findings to National Geographic, which led to further investigations. It was believed that the 1576 mass grave was caused by the Venetian plague that wreaked havoc across the country at the time. During medieval times, plague victims were commonly buried and then unburied as new bodies had to be added to the gravesites. Every now and then, gravediggers would find corpses that had blood seeping out of their mouths and noses. They believed these signs pointed to vampirism, and that the corpses were spreading the plague. They would then put bricks or rocks into their mouths to stop the plague from spreading further.

Bloody Appendices

OTHER CREATURES
OF THE NIGHT

There's nothing I'm afraid of like scared people.

—Robert Frost

Aye, we know there are many predators out there in the great, vast world. If we aren't worried about the zombie apocalypse, we are clutching our purses in fear of getting mugged. And thanks to medication, many of us who might stay up all night wrought with anxiety can get some sleep. I can't tell you that what you are about to read is going to help ease any of those fears. In fact, it may add to them. In addition to the usual ghosts that rattle the windows and the demons that lurk in the basement, you can now add the following to your list of things you'd rather not encounter in the night.

Bogle [BOGGLE, BOGILL, BOGEY, BOOGIE, BOOGIEMAN]

A bogle is a Scottish ghost or folkloric being, also sometimes known as a boggle or a bogill. Its name is derived from the same Middle English word *bugge* that our modern boogieman shares its origins with. But while the boogieman can be almost-spotted lurking under the beds and behind the closet doors of unsuspecting young children whose parents have lured them to bed on the pretense that no such thing as a boogieman exists, the death bogle tends to stay out-of-doors, usually near crossroads and creepy trees.

Though in theory you might find it tempting to assure your young children the boogieman is not real, please take heed. There are no circumstances in which you should think that a bogey, aka the death bogle, sounds "cool" or "interesting" enough to set out to see exactly what one looks like, or that you should make the foolish mistake that one is actually harmless, or worse, "doesn't exist." How often has a boogieman scenario led to the death of, or at least the terror of, poor children who foolishly believe their parents can protect them? Without a supernatural statistician on staff, we'll have to rely on the many incidents that parents soothe away saying it was only a dream—or rather, only a nightmare. But what about those who inadvertently "forget" the warnings

given by the locals and their loved ones and dare enter the crossroads in search of the death bogle? The rate of death is 100 percent. Worse even than a gypsy curse or voodoo hex, a sighting of the death bogle (if meant for you) will result in your demise. Guaranteed.

CHANGELINGS

Today's parent is an informed parent. From checkups to child locks, the modern mom and dad do everything they can to ensure that their little one will be safe and happy. So it is a shame that so many parents are completely unaware of one of the biggest threats to babies out there: fairies. Yes, babies are of particular interest to fairies, and the wicked fae will often stop at nothing to get their hands on a precious little bundle.

Many a parent has been tricked by the Queen of the Fairies, whose orders result in switching a creature from another realm for their human counterpart. When a sweet and robust baby goes ill, losing her cheerful demeanor and coloring, perhaps developing a nasty cough that rattles the cradle, this is the result of a changeling. When a calm and cuddly newborn becomes fussy and cries all hours of the night, it isn't colic, as so many foolish parents suspect. It is much more likely to be the offspring of a foul troll or lovely pixie, switched with the sleeping babe while the exhausted parents slept.

On the subject of changelings, William Butler Yeats writes the following:

> Sometimes the fairies fancy mortals, and carry them away into their own country, leaving instead some sickly fairy child, or a log of wood so bewitched that it seems to be a mortal pining away, and dying, and being buried. Most commonly they steal children. If you "over look a child," that is look on it with envy, the fairies have it in their power. Many things can be done to find out in a child a changeling, but there is one infallible thing—lay it on the fire with this formula, "Burn, burn, burn—if of the devil, burn; but if of God and the saints, be safe from harm" (given by Lady Wilde). Then if it be a changeling it will rush up the chimney with a cry, for, according to Giraldus Cambrensis, "fire is the greatest of enemies to every sort of phantom, in so much that those who have seen apparitions fall into a swoon as soon as they are sensible of the brightness of fire."

GOBLINS

There is a great deal of debate on the subject of goblins and whether or not they are menacing, not to mention strictly nocturnal. In his massive exploration of Welsh folklore, William Wirt Sikes writes that he believes the word *goblin* perhaps derived from the word *coblyn* or *Coblynau*—a class of fairy which haunt mines and underground caves and are characterized by their knocking. These are most commonly known to us as Tommyknockers. They do have something in common with brownies and hobgoblins—often helpful creatures who hang around the house and aid in housework, so long as they are fed regularly. Sikes also writes about a good-natured goblin called the Boobach, which has an undeserved reputation for causing harm. Some people consider *goblin* a general term for fairies of a wide variety.

POOKAS

Also known as the *Puca*, the Irish word for "goblin," you can find as many variations of spelling as different forms of the pooka itself: Pook, Puki, Puka, Phouka, Pwca, Pwwka, Púka, and even Puk or Puck (it certainly bears some relation to the infamous Puck in its trickery and Pan-like behavior). The Pooka can take nearly any form, including invisibility, though it is most frequently sighted in the form of a horse—a black horse with eyes of fire and breath of blue flame. This horse takes the terrified mortal who is most unfortunate to have encountered it on a midnight ride and turns his hair white, but no real harm actually comes to the person, usually. The shapeshifter can also appear as a goat, goblin, dog, and even a rabbit. Remember that big invisible rabbit that James Stewart spent a good deal of time conversing and sometimes even arguing with in the 1950 film *Harvey*? Harvey, the 6-foot-3.5-inch-tall white rabbit was a Pooka.

Stewart's character Elwood P. Dowd was a drunk. This is another recurring theme in encounters with a Pooka. Victims are usually drunk and stumbling home in the dead of night when they see it. (I must admit I've been a prime candidate for the Pooka's trickery on more than one occasion myself. Although my Pooka most recently took the form of Cookie Monster. It was a very long night.)

This generally works perfectly with the Pooka's plan to torment its victim—no one believes the drunk. And though the Pooka today is generally more trickster, loving nothing more than a good scare to its victim, it does possess the ability to be more vicious. Once thought to be responsible, along with other malevolent spirits, for such ill luck as blighted corn, sour milk, and sick children, the Pooka seems to mostly cause those who are evil of heart to take their own lives— leaping from cliffs to rocks below, firing guns to the chest, and the like.

Varla Ventura

A lover of all things freaky and terrifying, Varla Ventura lives in a creaky, haunted attic of an old Victorian in San Francisco, California where—when not burning the midnight oil writing about weird news—she can be seen traversing the hidden cemeteries and phantom ships in the Bay Area.

BUCKET [OF BLOOD] LISTS

We're all familiar with the term Bucket List, but why not start your own Bucket of Blood List? The following will get you started on your list of must-sees and must-reads on the topics of banshees, werewolves, and vampires (and a few other creatures that go bump in the night!). Disclaimer: This isn't even close to being a complete list, but it's a good start.

Banshee Movies

Banshee!!! (2008): A group of college students is killed by a creature that can make them hallucinate through sound waves. It's not entirely accurate about banshees, but borrows from the folklore.

Cry of the Banshee (1970): In Elizabethan England, a wicked, witch-hunting Lord kills almost all the members of a coven of witches. Their leader, Oona, sicks a banshee on him. Pros: The witches aren't the bad guys, and the film takes on the horrible witch hunts, looking at things from the more uncommon angle. Cons: This movie's banshee bears little resemblance to the banshees of folklore and myth.

Darby O'Gill and the Little People (1959): An Irish tale about a father's pride, mischievous leprechaun magic, and young love (with a banshee grim reaper to boot!).

Ju-On (2002): Divided into six shorter films, this is the original Japanese story that the American film *The Grudge* is based upon. Similarly, it follows a curse that occupies a house in Japan and brings terror and despair to those who dwell within, and senses their dread when they hear the death rattle of the banshee.

Scream of the Banshee (2011): In this horror thriller, after a college professor opens a banshee box, everyone who heard the scream is killed one by one.

Smallville, episode 189, "Escape" (2010): Clark Kent and Lois Lane head to a bed-and-breakfast for a romantic getaway and encounter the DC Comics character the Silver Banshee—the cursed Siobhan McDougal, whose familial past created a lust for revenge and a hatred of men.

So Weird, episode 24, "Banshee" (1999): The show's protagonist, Fiona, encounters a banshee and fears the impending death of her grandfather.

The Grudge (2004): This American remake of the Japanese film *Ju-On* tells the story of Karen Davis, an unsuspecting exchange student who takes a job as a caregiver of a house. Of course, the home is haunted by a dark curse, manifested by the spirit of a dead housewife whose rage and sorrow allow her to haunt the house and claim her victims.

The White Lady (2006): A young girl seeks acceptance from her school friends at an arts academy and discovers a dark secret that binds them together.

WEREWOLF MOVIES

An American Werewolf in London (1981): American tourists encounter a werewolf in England.

An American Werewolf in Paris (1997): An American tourist becomes involved in a werewolf plot to overcome the power of the moon.

Blood and Chocolate (2007): Vivian, a teenage werewolf, falls in love with a human and risks exposing her family's secret. Based on a book with the same name.

Buffy the Vampire Slayer, episode 27, "Phases" (1998): A close friend of Buffy, Willow Rosenberg, finds out that her boyfriend is a werewolf.

Dog Soldiers (2002): Werewolves wreak havoc on a military platoon.

Ginger Snaps (2000): Two sisters' lives change forever when one is bitten by a werewolf.

Harry Potter and the Deathly Hallows, Part II (2011): Harry Potter and his friends battle Lord Voldemort and his evil forces, including the ferocious and cruel werewolf Fenrir Greyback.

Hemlock Grove (2012): A young girl's brutal murder triggers an investigation into a town that hides dark secrets, including a werewolf.

Red Riding Hood (2011): A spin on the classic *Little Red Riding Hood* tells the story of a young woman whose town lives in fear of a blood-thirsty wolf that has terrorized it for years.

Silver Bullet (1985): Marty Coslaw's town is being attacked by a werewolf.

Strippers vs. Werewolves (2012): A man is killed in a strip club and becomes a werewolf on the next full moon.

Teen Wolf (1985): A high school student discovers he's a werewolf. Michael J. Fox is the lead. Seriously, this is a classic!

The Company of Wolves (1984): Young Rosaleen learns about werewolves and their intentions with innocent maidens who fall victim to their spell.

The Howling (1981): A newswoman is sent to a rehabilitation center after a brush with death and finds that the terror continues when she realizes that the other patients are out for blood.

The Wolf Man (1941): For werewolf films, this sets the bar. Starring Lon Chaney Jr. as the lead character, it also stars Bela Lugosi as a fellow werewolf.

The Wolf Man (2010): A revamped retelling of the 1941 classic, the film tells the story of a man who returns home and is bitten by a werewolf.

Werewolf, featured on *Mystery Science Theater* (1996): An archaeologist is scratched by an ancient werewolf skeleton and becomes a werewolf himself.

Vampire Movies

Abraham Lincoln: Vampire Hunter (2012): A founding father has a secret identity as a vampire hunter. Based on the novel of the same name.

Bram Stoker's Dracula (1973 & 1992): Both are based on Bram Stoker's 1897 Gothic novel *Dracula*, which tells the story of Count Dracula, a vampire who is hunted by Van Helsing as he attempts to make a home for himself in England. The 1973 version is a made-for-TV movie starring Jack Palance.

Buffy the Vampire Slayer (1992): A sassy cheerleader fulfills her destiny as one of the world's vampire slayers. This movie inspired the hit television series.

Cirque du Freak: The Vampire's Assistant (2009): Based on the *Vampire Blood* trilogy from Darren Shan, in this movie, there's a traveling freak show *and* vampires. Need I say more?

Dark Shadows: A gothic soap opera that aired from 1966 to 1971, *Dark Shadows* centered around the Collins family and Barnabas

Collins, the vampire. Werewolves, zombies, monsters, witches, warlocks, and time travel were among the supernatural topics. In 2012, director Tim Burton made a film based on the central family and starring Johnny Depp as Barnabas Collins.

Daybreakers (2009): A futuristic world overrun by vampires, with William Defoe as a recovered human trying to reverse the curse.

Dracula (1931): The end-all, be-all of vampire movies. If you've never seen this, get thee to your instant queue and get watching. Bela Lugosi plays perfectly the iconic, tormented Dracula, in heart-breakingly gorgeous black and white. Don't even bother seeing any other movies on this list if you haven't seen this one.

Fright Night (1985): A teenage boy realizes his neighbor is a vampire.

Hotel Transylvania (2012): Dracula owns a hotel in Transylvania and invites Frankenstein's monster, a mummy, a werewolf family, and the Invisible Man to celebrate his daughter's 118th birthday. Animated, funny, and adorable.

Interview with a Vampire: The Vampire Chronicles (1994): Louis de Pointe du Lac is interviewed by a reporter who attempts to discover the truth about Louis, his maker Lestat, and other vampires in the world.

League of Extraordinary Gentlemen (2003): Based on the graphic novel series of the same name, the film brings together a cast of the Victorian era's most notorious and revered characters to protect the world against unknown terror. Among them is Mina Harker, the character made famous by Bram Stoker.

Lemora: A Child's Tale of the Supernatural (1973): Upon returning to her hometown to say goodbye to her dying father, a young woman gets involved with vampires and witches.

Let the Right One In (2008): A bullied twelve-year-old boy develops a friendship with a vampire child in a Stockholm suburb. Based on a creepy 2004 Swedish novel by the same name.

Lifeforce (1985): Vampires from outer space invade London.

Near Dark (1987): Caleb meets Mae, a beautiful, mysterious drifter whose bite changes him into a vampire.

Nosferatu (1922): This revered German Expressionist film follows the vampire Count Orlok and his reign of terror on a neighboring village.

Not of This Earth (1988): Mixing the sci-fi and horror genres, this film brings a vampire from outer space face-to-face with humans on Earth.

Queen of the Damned (2002): The film follows the vampire Lestat and the first vampire, Akasha, who is awakened and possesses an unquenchable thirst.

Taste the Blood of Dracula (1970): Three men bring Dracula back to life and kill one of his faithful servants. Count Dracula seeks revenge.

The Lost Boys (1987): Two brothers move to California with their mom and suspect that their new town is home to dangerous vampires.

The Munsters (1964-1966): This CBS television comedy was a black-and-white throwback to the Bela Lugosi era of films with a family, the Munsters, living in a creaky mansion à la the Addams Family. But unlike the Addams Family, who were horror-loving goths, the Munsters were a family of blue-collar monsters. The Grandpa character, aka Sam Dracula, was made legendary by actor Al Lewis. Mel Blanc, best known as the voice of Bugs Bunny, made occasional cameos as The Raven.

The Nude Vampire (1970): Georges Radamante leads a suicide cult and seeks immortality through a connection with a vampire woman.

The Twilight Saga (2008–2012): Trilogy of movies based on Stephenie Meyer's bestselling series including a triangle of mortal, vampire, and werewolf.

The Vampire Diaries (2009): A supernatural drama set in the fictional small town of Mystic Falls, Virgina, that centers around Elena Gilbert, her malevolent doppelgänger, and two vampire brothers.

True Blood (2008): Based on Charlaine Harris' *The Southern Vampire Mysteries* books, this television series depicts the adventures of Sookie Stackhouse, a telepathic waitress, in Bon Temps, Louisiana, and the co-existence of vampires and humans.

Underworld series (2003–2012): This series of movies begins when vampire soldier Selene battles to defend the life of a human who finds himself in the middle of a war between vampires and werewolves.

Van Helsing (2004): Count Dracula's nemesis returns to a world of vampires, Dr. Frankenstein's monster, and a deadly werewolf.

BOOKIE WOOKS!

My fellow creature lover and friend Kat of *katlovesbooks.blogspot.com* supplied me with this supernatural list of recommended reading.

Vampires

13 Bullets by David Wellington
30 Days of Night by Steve Niles
A Discovery of Witches by Deborah Harkness
Abraham Lincoln: Vampire Hunter by Seth Grahame-Smith
Blood of Eden series by Julie Kagawa
Bloodlines series by Richelle Mead
Blue Bloods series by Melissa de la Cruz
Children of the Night by Dan Simmons
Dracula Continues series by Elaine Bergstrom
Drink, Slay, Love by Sarah Beth Durst
Evernight series by Claudia Gray
House of Night series by P.C. Cast

Interview with the Vampire by Anne Rice
Jaz Parks series by Jennifer Rardin
Jessica series by Beth Fantaskey
Let the Right One In by John Ajvide Lindqvist
Salem's Lot by Stephen King
Sunshine by Robin McKinley
The Chronicles of Vladimir Tod series by Heather Brewer
The Coldest Girl in Coldtown by Holly Black
The Delicate Dependency by Michael Talbot
The Historian by Elizabeth Kostova
The Hunger by Whitley Streiber
The Morganville Vampires series by Rachel Caine
The Sookie Stackhouse series by Charlaine Harris
The Vampire Academy series by Richelle Mead
The Vampire Diaries by L.J. Smith
The Vampire's Promise by Caroline B. Cooney
Twilight series by Stephenie Meyer

Werewolves

Alpha & Omega series by Patricia Briggs
Blood and Chocolate by Annette Curtis Klause
Darkness Rising series by Kelley Armstrong
Nightshade series by Andrea Cremer
Sisters Red by Jackson Pearce
The Last Werewolf by Glen Duncan
The Wolves of Mercy Falls by Maggie Steifvater
Wolf Moon by Charles de Lint

Banshees

Soul Screamers series by Rachel Vincent

Dark Fairies

Fairyland series by Catherine M. Valente
Fever series by Karen Marie Moning
Modern Faerie Tales series by Holly Black
The Iron Fey series by Julie Kagawa
The Wild Wood by Charles de Lint
Wings series by Aprilynne Pike

Ghosts

Anna series by Kendare Blake
Revenants series by Amy Plum
Shades of London series by Maureen Johnson
Tamsin by Peter S. Beagle
The Body Finder series by Kimberly Derting
The Diviners by Libba Bray
The Graveyard Book by Neil Gaiman
The Raven Boys by Maggie Stiefvater

VOLUMES OF FORGOTTEN LORE

Many of the short stories in this book were first published in collections from the late 19th and early 20th centuries. If you enjoyed the strange collections of folklore and terrifying tales of true encounters in this book, you may find the following books of great interest. They are very tricky to find in original form, but reproductions abound and *gutenburg.org* offers many of these as free ebooks to the reader willing to slog through strange formatting.

British Goblins: Welsh Folk-Lore, Fairy Mythology, Legends and Traditions by William Wirt Sikes (1880)
Dracula's Guest and Other Weird Stories by Bram Stoker (1914)

Fairy and Folk Tales of Irish Peasantry by W.B. Yeats (1888)

Ghostly Tales, Volume 5 by J.S. Le Fanu (1870)

Irish Wonders: The Ghosts, Giants, Pookas, Demons, Leprechauns, Banshees, Fairies, Witches, Widows, Old Maids, and Other Marvels by D.R. McAnally Jr. (1888)

The Banshee by Elliott O'Donnell (1920)

The Best Ghost Stories by Arthur B. Reeve (1919)

The Book of Scottish Ghost Stories by Elliott O'Donnell (1911)

The Book of Were-Wolves by Sabine Baring-Gould (1865)

The House of the Vampire by George Sylvester Viereck (1907)

The Second Book of Tales by Eugene Field (1911)

The Vampyre, A Tale by John William Polidori (1819)

Werwolves by Elliott O'Donnell (1912)

SOURCES

Bartlett, John. *Bartlett's Book of Familiar Quotations, Sixteenth Edition: Justin Kaplan, Ed.* Boston: Little, Brown and Company, 1992.

Biggs, Mary. *The Columbia Book of Quotations by Women.* New York: Columbia University Press, 1996.

Buckland, Raymond. *The Weiser Field Guide to Ghosts.* San Francisco: Weiser Books, 2009.

Dixon, J.M. *The Weiser Field Guide to Vampires.* San Francisco: Weiser Books, 2009.

Editors, The Readers Digest Association. *The Reader's Digest Great Encyclopedic Dictionary*, Pleasantville, New York: The Reader's Digest Association, 1967.

Schutt, Bill. *Dark Banquet, Blood and the Curious Lives of Blood-Feeding Creatures.* New York: Harmony Books, 2008.

Sebastiaan, Father. *Vampyre Sanguinomicon.* San Francisco: Weiser Books, 2010.

———. *Vampyre Magick.* San Francisco: Weiser Books, 2012.

Ventura, Varla. *The Book of the Bizarre.* San Francisco: Weiser Books, 2008.

———. *Beyond Bizarre.* San Francisco: Weiser Books, 2010.

ONLINE SOURCES

alam25.tripod.com

coopandcottage.blogspot.com

crazyhorsesghost.hubpages.com

facts.randomhistory.com

ghostvillage.com

gods-and-monsters.com

goodreads.com

hellhorror.com

ilovewerewolves.com

irelandseye.com

kens5.com/news

mahalo.com

monstropedia.org

news.google.com

news.nationalgeographic.com

newser.com

nytimes.com

paranormal.lovetoknow.com/Real_Vampire_Sightings

pbs.org

prairieghosts.com

science.howstuffworks.com/science-vs-myth

sfgate.com

squidoo.com/real-history-of-vampires

varlaventura.wordpress.com (The Blog of the Bizarre)

werewolf-news.com
wikipedia.org
wookiepedia.com
yourirish.com

ACKNOWLEDGMENTS

My deepest gratitude to the many friends who have kept me company through the wee hours of the night, in particular: Pirate Chris, Gem Blade, Heinz the Magnificent, Lia, Lizzy Lee Savage, The Vinyl Avenger, Lucy Lee, Lorian, Abby, Rowen, Little Buddy, Alix, Chris A., and Dee.

Special thanks to Chris Hatfield for his vast knowledge of obscure and awesome films, and for being a general all-around inspiration.

Thanks to my family, who have often kept me up through the night: Ken, Henrik, Emma, Ida, Aurora, Jacob, Debbie, Dina, Philly, Sabrina, Wendy, Ethan, Corrine, Dolores, Andy, Sandy, Norm, Donn, Fran (who taught me to swim in the ocean), Andy II, Sue, and Steve.

Much gratitude to the Red Wheel Weiser Team: Vanessa Ta, Jordan Overby, Kim Ehart, Jan Johnson, Caroline Pincus, Pat Rose, Greg Brandenburgh, Jim

Warner, Bonni Hamilton, Nicole Deneka, Michael Kerber, Sylvia Hopkins, Dennis Fitzgerald, amazing copyeditor Julia "Bloody Appendices" Campbell, and stellar designer Debby "Design-Diva" Dutton. Super big thanks to my incredible publicist Kat Salazar who knows the best places to pitch a freak like me. Special thanks to darling intern Katie Dalia who helped wrangle me in. Most of all, thanks to my incredible editor, Amber Guetebier, without whom this book could not exist: you are an inspiration and more adept at creature-research and wild nights than I could ever hope to be. I owe you a Screaming Banshee.

The trouble with sleep is the going to and the coming from.

—BOB KAUFMAN

TO OUR READERS